The Lessons

MELANIE MCALLESTER

spinsters ink
minneapolis, mn

First edition
10-9-8-7-6-5-4-3-2-1

Spinsters Ink
P.O. Box 300170
Minneapolis, MN 55403-5170

Cover Art and Design by: Lois Stanfield, LightSource Images
Production: Melanie Cockrell   Lori Loughney
             Lynette D'Amico   Rhonda Lundquist
             Joan Drury   Lou Ann Matossian
             Cynthia Fogard   Stefanie Shiffler
             Kelly Kager   Liz Tufte
             Carolyn Law

This is a work of fiction. Any similarity to actual events, or persons
living or dead is a coincidence.

Library of Congress Cataloging-in-Publication Data
McAllester, Melanie, 1962 –
The lessons / by Melanie McAllester—1st ed.
            p.   cm.
ISBN 0-933216-99-8 (acid-free paper) : $9.95
    1. Lesbians—California, Northern—Crimes against—Fiction.
    2. Policewomen—California, Northern—Fiction.
    3. Rape—California, Northern—Fiction.   I. Title.
PS3563.C266L47   1994
813′ .54—dc20   94-2770
                                                    CIP

Printed in the U.S.A. on recycled acid-free paper.

Acknowledgments

There's no shade, the sun is beating down, and our short little hike is actually a climb up the side of a mountain. I should have known better when she said I might find the excursion "a little challenging." My competitiveness is the only thing which keeps me at her side, trying hard not to let my gasps for air give me away.

She decides to start a conversation. A not-so-subtle attempt to demonstrate her superior endurance. "So, what are you going to do, now that you've finished school?"

"Well." I pause to catch my breath and give up on not sounding winded. After all, I'm still walking—that's a good thing. "Now don't laugh at me."

Barb gives me one of those looks. She always takes everybody seriously. I continue, "I'm going to write a book. I've already got the characters and most of the outline done."

"Really? That's great. You know I want to do that some time. Hey, I could help you by editing."

Barb's quick mind is sprinting ahead with ideas and dreams about new careers and her pace quickens. Great! Just what I needed, to go faster up this mountain. Although by the time we reach the top, her enthusiasm and confidence have rubbed off, and no task seems impossible.

▼

Thanks so much to Barbara Bond who let me create and carefully guided me through transforming my police report style into a novel. I am sure that if she had not worked with me this book would have never been published. From that first moment to the end, she always encouraged and assisted me to make my work better each time I write. I hope that someday I can do the same for her.

Thanks also to Cathy whose excitement kept me working even when I felt it was a waste of time.

▼

Most of this book was written in a special home on Dartmouth Avenue. This house was filled with women I will always be close to, even though our bond is difficult to describe. They were patient with me when I spent hours writing in my room with the door closed, writing in the morning, in the afternoon, and sometimes late into the night. They understood when I didn't always carry my load of the many household chores; only occasionally did I get my "we need to talk" dinner conversation openers. Even then, they had good reminders about not letting my writing consume my entire life.

Thanks to Tammy, Alana, and Lynn. Special thanks to Lacey who helped me to really believe that everything in life does happen for a reason. Maybe that's why our friendship endures through all the turmoil. It means more to me than she may realize.

▼

"Say something to her." Lisa's whispered instructions are emphasized by a gentle shove. "We didn't come up here for nothing." Her low voice pushes a little harder.

"Give me a second. What am I going to say?" My shyness is overwhelming.

"Come on, we practiced in the car. Just say what we talked about." She gives me one last shove.

We were at the San Francisco Book Fair to meet anybody from Spinsters, where my book was under consideration, and Lisa wasn't about to let me sneak from their booth without even an effort. I finally worked up the courage to say something and introduced myself to Kelly Kager. She promised she would move my book to the top of her pile, and a few days later I got a call from Spinsters.

Thanks to Lisa Talbott for always being there in the last few years. We once promised each other that when one was in need of strength, the other would provide it—I'm glad that this has never changed. I'm looking forward to my 55th birthday!

▼

When I write my thank-yous, how can I not mention my families—both of them? First, there are my friends and peers at PAPD, people who have stood by me in more difficult situations than many could imagine. I want to mention some names, but all my fellow officers should know that they've helped create the impressions which contribute to this book. Special thanks to Carole and Bill Baldwin: I'm counting on you two to help me through all the other stuff that goes with being published. Sandra Brown: my bad publishing sister, you make me proud. Mike Honiker: you and I know the truth. John Costa: your leadership and friendship are appreciated. Larry Peterson: you told me I could do anything and maybe you were right. Plus Pete, Reba, Cindi, Mark, Patty, Kathy, Lori, and everybody else that puts up with me.

Then there's my family. There is really not much to say that they have not heard before. I love them all, and I'm so lucky to have a family I like, too. You all are my friends, my trustees, and a part of my soul. I love you, Mom, Dad, Jeff, Liz, Greg, Heather, Sam, and Erin. Without all of you, my work would mean nothing.

▼

Thanks to Robbi and Sandy who have celebrated each step of success with me and kept me from going crazy when my life was not filled with only happy moments. You two are great friends.

Thanks to Devi Stanford for making me smile, laugh, and finally relax, at least a little.

Thanks to Kelly Kager for actually digging my book out of the pile and reading it. Thanks also for all the encouragement along the way.

Thanks to everybody at Spinsters Ink for helping to make my dream come true.

Prologue

Struggling back to consciousness, her body was still peaceful while her mind tried urgently to extract itself from sleep and focus on its surroundings. She felt herself awakening, not really understanding why. Her eyes opened, and instantly she was alert. Quickly her mind took control of her body. She had heard something. At least she thought she remembered the sound of breaking glass, but was it a dream? She sat still, holding her breath and concentrating as she listened for other sounds.

Nothing.

What was it that had disrupted her sleep; what was still disturbing her now?

It had been a day of stifling heat. Even now it felt like mid-afternoon. Many people were probably still awake and outside, trying to cool themselves. Maybe it had been a neighbor or an animal. More likely she was just imagining something. A fictitious sound from a dream that was lost to memory the instant she awoke. Once again she listened and heard nothing unusual.

Lying back down, she laughed at herself for being paranoid. She was not used to being the only person in the house. Thinking back to childhood, she remembered believing that each shadow outside her curtains was the "boogie man." The night light provided by her father had helped.

She forced herself to laugh again and spoke out to the darkness, "Maybe I need a night light now." The sound of her own voice started to relax her in preparation for sleep to return.

▼

A noise *inside* the house! Footsteps in the hall outside her room. She hadn't been dreaming, mistaken, or foolish. Her mind had tried to warn her, and she had brushed it off as a child asking a million "why" questions. This time she was awake and sure of what she had heard.

Could she make it to the door and lock it? She started to move slowly towards the door. Simultaneously the door's knob began to turn. The sight momentarily turned her to stone while her mind shifted from thought to instinct. Fight or flight. She crumpled back down into her bed and pulled around her the covers which had been flung to the floor in the heat. She chose to feign sleep. A feeble flight, but it was her only chance. Let this person take everything while she attempted to imitate the calm of sleep.

The door creaked an eerie warning as it opened. She wanted to sit up and scream, but instead she lay still. Her mind was creating frightful images of a shadow of a human approaching with a deadly weapon in hand. What if this person was going to kill her? She would not even see it coming. Her mind began to put a face to the person who was in her room. Every killer in every horror movie she had ever seen was suddenly standing in her room. The fear she felt convinced her that her life was about to end. Still, she forced herself not to move, reasoning it would be better not to know if she was indeed about to die.

▼

He stood outside the door of the bedroom he thought was hers. Black wool pants and a black wool sweater caused him to sweat profusely. The black ski mask and black leather gloves would assure that his identity would remain unknown. Although he hated this outfit, it was crucial to his safety. The fact that he was more experienced made him smile with confidence. He had gotten good at this little hobby of his.

The first attack had been motivated by an unpredicted opportunity. There had been little planning and therefore he was sure evidence had been left all over the house. He had even been stupid enough to enter the house without first putting on his gloves or ski mask. However, he had caught his mistake and wiped the area clean of fingerprints. He had also forgotten the mask in the rental car, but it would probably never be found.

Tonight his strategy had been flawless. The rental car would never be noticed simply because it blended into the neighborhood. There were similar cars parked in all the driveways, and rental agencies no longer placed stickers on their vehicles for fear of making their customers easy targets for ruthless street criminals. As he had silently approached his target from blocks away, there was no disturbance, not even a barking dog. The shadows of all the beautifully planted front yards made him practically invisible to anybody passing on the street. But nobody had passed. The heat was so oppressive that in this neighborhood residents were not venturing from the comfort of their air-conditioned homes. Even when he broke the little pane of glass on the rear door of the house nobody seemed to have noticed. No lights had come on. No doors opened. Nobody risked a confrontation with the heat.

Now luck remained on his side as he found the bedroom door unlocked. This one was going to be easy. He walked into the room and saw her lying still in the bed. She was pretending to sleep, yet her chest rose and fell like storm waves moving across the ocean. Her breathing sent thunderclaps of fear crashing throughout her body.

Silently he walked across the room. Her bed had a thick white quilt over it and she had it wrapped around herself. He felt anger stir as he realized white was not right for this dyke. Women who stole other women from men did not deserve to wrap themselves in the innocence and security of white. He quickly leaned over and forced his hand across her mouth as he removed a gag from his pocket.

"Sorry, honey—this ain't no burglary."

She bolted from her nightmare, sitting straight up in bed. The gray tank top which she always wore to bed clung to her breasts as sweat rolled slowly down her chest. Well-defined muscles were taut and ready to take on the images that lingered in her mind. Her long legs now craved movement, instantly cramping from the sudden release of energy.

Slowly she stretched her legs to relieve the pain and then got out of bed and walked out on her balcony, seeking fresh air. The heat made the outdoors as confining as her bedroom. She found it difficult to breathe and could not get her body to relax. Her mind was already straining to analyze her nightmare, and her body was just going to have to wait.

Of course, Elizabeth Mendoza did not need to analyze anything. After almost ten years in law enforcement she knew when she awoke like this something horrible had happened. Tonight she dreaded discovering that another woman had been attacked.

Although she was a homicide investigator, her Captain had asked her to assist in the investigation of a serial rapist who was attacking only lesbians. He had asked her, he said, because the suspect was a definite psycho and apt to kill somebody soon.

She knew it was because she was a lesbian and the department wanted to make sure they were being as sensitive as possible to the victims.

The reason why she was on these cases didn't matter. She had to get this idiot off the streets. She felt as if her friends, her community, everybody was relying on her. She couldn't let them down after having let so many down before, both professionally and personally. Her mind started to drift to all those things she had promised herself were part of her past and nothing else. The lost love, the lost confidence, the struggle to go on with her life. It was all behind her now, and she wanted it to remain there.

Snapping around, she marched back into her room, not about to spend one more sleepless night reliving what she couldn't change. She walked over to her dresser and removed a fresh gray Jockey tank top from the drawer. She took off her drenched one, being careful not to aggravate her already tense muscles. The fresh top fit snugly on her upper body due to her etched definition, giving the impression of somebody who worked hard to look good. But the truth was, she was lucky and lazy because her body was a gift of good genes.

The fresh top felt like a gentle caress from the right woman as it slid down her upper body. She picked up the glass of water which had been ice when she went to bed and allowed herself a big messy gulp, most of which ended up running down her neck to her chest. The coolness of the water finally allowed her to relax somewhat.

Crawling back into bed, she tried to force everything from her mind. A restless sleep had finally returned when the telephone rang. Startled, she snatched it as if shutting off the morning alarm, but sleep was still invading her mind and she forgot to say anything.

"Tenny, Tenny, are you there?"

"Yes, I'm sorry. Is that you, Martin?"

"Get in here, the bastard hit again. These are your cases now, no more assisting bullshit. We got the call from the victim at 0326 hours. She's already had her rape exam and we're bringing her back from the hospital now. She'll be waiting for you."

"All right, travel time."

Tenny hung up the phone. Over the years she had developed a well-known reputation for working a case from every angle. Turning it inside out. Dissecting it. Whatever it took. No matter how much time was required. She stuck with cases until the guilty person went to prison. Sergeant Martin had been the first to describe her investigative style as pure tenacity and started calling her Tenny. Now everybody called her Tenny, including her family and friends.

Tonight Tenny was struggling with herself, feeling somewhat adrift as she quickly dressed to go interview the third victim in two months. This suspect had already damaged so many lives, and they still weren't close to catching him. She didn't want to face another victim. Didn't want this woman to search her eyes for the answers. Tenny didn't have any. She couldn't cope with letting another person down. Once before she had come up a little short and somebody had paid with their life.

As Tenny finished dressing she put on her gun and badge. With the badge came the strength she had momentarily lacked. It was the shield behind which Elizabeth could take protection as Tenny started the investigation on *her* rape cases.

▼

Tenny stopped outside the interview room not knowing exactly how to proceed. It had been a long time since she had done the initial interview of a rape victim. She had done follow-up interviews with some of the prior victims, but by then they had calmed and their pain had dulled somewhat. In Homicide, of course, none of the victims had ever spoken a word. Instead she had dealt with distraught family members and sometimes

7

the killers themselves. But that wasn't the same as dealing with a living, breathing *victim*. Rape victims were the hardest. No crime was more personal. No crime was more devastating. Women always felt they could have done something, even if it meant giving up their lives in a fight.

Tenny tried to prepare herself to become part of the emotional turmoil the rapist had left in his wake. The woman in the interview room would be struggling to make sense of what had happened, searching for answers. Tenny knew she could not provide them, not now, probably not ever. Yet she could be the start of the healing process for this victim, and she needed to have herself together before entering the room.

Apprehensive and angry, Tenny wanted answers.

Tenny swept her dark, thick hair back from her face, stood up straight and lifted herself from the last remnants of sleep. She had thrown on a pair of her favorite jeans, a plain gray sweatshirt and her ass-kicking cowgirl boots. They always made her feel comfortable and confident. She focused on this feeling. This was her investigation now and she was going to find him.

Ready to be strong, Tenny stepped into the room, took one look at the victim, and all her well-intended preparation slipped from her as though she had been deflated.

The woman sat at the table posed as if she were about to conduct a business interview. Her hands were clasped in front of her, her shoulders squared and her legs politely crossed. She gave Tenny a brief smile as she entered the room. For a moment she looked like she was about to greet Tenny with a warm and gracious "hello." The desperate display of strength lasted only seconds. Then the smile faded as mental and physical exhaustion took over. A lost look came over her face, her effort to be strong melted.

The woman's eyes were red and puffy from the tears she still fought to control. Tenny looked into them as she drew closer and saw only emptiness and fear. The woman had been beaten up, but her bruises were only a mere token of the real damage that had been done. Tenny noticed that the woman was shaking in tight, constrained tremors. She was not frail, but at this moment the slightest amount of pressure would send her reeling.

"Hello, Kerry. I'm Tenny, and I will be investigating this case. Is there anybody I can call to be with you?"

"The other officer already offered. There's nobody."

Tenny sat across from Kerry, who would no longer look at Tenny. Already at a loss for words, Tenny felt guilty and embarrassed. She was a cop, part of a group of people that others relied on to protect them. Whenever she faced victims, she felt the weight of that responsibility settle heavily upon her. For Tenny, each victim represented another failure.

Tenny sat there for several minutes, struggling not to let her own emotions interfere with the investigation. She could feel the anger and frustration building inside her. If she could do nothing else for Kerry at this moment, she could share the strength that comes with anger.

Slowly Tenny moved her hand across the empty table between them towards Kerry's still clasped hands. As she touched Kerry, her hand was instantly engulfed by this woman's own hands. Her grip was unbelievable, the clutch of somebody fighting for her life. Tenny had not been prepared for the flood of memories which this grasp brought. Startled and confused, she almost pulled her hand away, but the transfusion of strength had already begun so she allowed it to continue.

▼

Kerry slowly lifted their arms towards her, creating a tripod on which she rested her head. Then the tears came again, this time in a steady stream. Finally she raised her head and looked into Tenny's eyes.

The image of a sunburnt chestnut came to Kerry—the ones at the top of the tree that have no protection from the intensity of the sun and are almost ready to drop. She had one of these trees in her backyard. The backyard of her home. The home she had worked so hard to obtain. The home she could never set foot in again.

Kerry's fear and fatigue evaporated in a storm of anger. "I thought he was going to kill me. I was ready to die. I wasn't prepared for what happened. That bastard took everything from me. He took my home, my peace of mind, my trust in what's right, my self-respect, and my body." Her voice was growing louder and her pain greater with each word.

"He did it as an act of prejudice. It wasn't for any kind of sexual satisfaction. It was to teach me what 'real love' was all about. That's what the fucker said. He wanted to 'make love' to me. To correct my misconceptions, to show me how nice it was to be with men. He kept saying that women shouldn't take other women from men."

Tenny had read about similar comments from the suspects in the other rape cases. This man's thrusting of values and morals onto others was completed by the ultimate form of intrusion.

"He didn't start to hurt me until I refused to make love to him. Can you believe it! He actually expected me to want to make love with him."

Then the question Tenny had been dreading came. "How can he think that what he's doing is right?"

Tenny hesitated, not knowing how to answer. "Both of us know that there are millions of people who think that how we live is wrong, people who would stop us if they could. Stop us from teaching in their schools, from attending their churches, from serving in their political offices. Stop us from being who we are. This guy thinks he can stop us by showing us *the way*. He can't stop what is just another way of expressing love. His hate is filtered through misconceptions, stereotypes, and ignorance. Our kind of love is pure and natural, which makes it stronger than his hate. Kerry, you're not wrong."

▼

Tenny felt completely drained after her interview. She needed to escape, to find a safe place to hide while her own emotions unraveled themselves. There was no hesitation on Tenny's part. She headed for home.

Now, as she pulled up in front of her parents' house, all the warmth and security of her childhood began to calm her frazzled nerves. Except for this one, Tenny had never really had a home. She had lived in several places and now even owned a house. Yet no place had ever really felt like *home*. They were just locations where she always felt a little lost, just places to stay while she searched for a home, searched for the love which had filled the house in which she had grown up. Once, she had come close—so close.

Tenny stepped through the front door and escaped from the uncertainty of the world. Here everything was secure: the portrait of her grandfather, the classical music in the background, and her parents' love. There were no surprises. Tenny was safe.

A familiar voice drifted through the halls from the kitchen, where her mother sat talking on the telephone. Tenny leaned against the counter, guessing that her oldest brother was on the other end of the line. Even this scene was a ritual. At least once a week Mom would call each of the children for a weekly update. Then she would relay any new information about the other kids. The five siblings never really *needed* to talk to each other, they just had to call Mom. They affectionately referred to her as Mother-Central. Smiling to herself, Tenny opened the door to the back workshop and stepped through into her father's place of escape.

He was seated at the work table with his glasses perfectly balanced on the end of his nose as he constructed another mobile. He would spend hours on the coast and in the forest, collecting nature's trinkets for his art.

He looked up at his youngest daughter as she walked through the door. "Ah, look at what the bay breeze blew through my door."

"Hi, Dad. Is this one for me?" Tenny asked as she sat down on the bench next to him.

"They're all for you, if you like." He went back to work. Tenny never stopped by unannounced unless something really good or really bad had just happened. The weary, sad look in his baby's eyes told him which it was this time. The two of them sat silently for no other reason than just to be there.

A few minutes later Tenny's mother came in and placed her hand on Tenny's forehead. "Are you sick? You look so pale."

Tenny laughed. "Mom, you know I stopped coming home to be taken care of when I was sick. I haven't done that for at least two years."

"Uh-huh, and when was the last time you were sick?"

Tenny shrugged her shoulders as if she wasn't sure. "Maybe about two years ago." They all laughed and Tenny knew she had done the right thing by coming home.

Her mother let everyone enjoy the happiness for a few moments and then launched into the subject which she knew had brought her Elizabeth home. She knew that Tenny wouldn't bring it up. Even here where she felt safest, she wouldn't allow weakness to show.

"Was there another rape last night?"

"Yeah, the same guy. They've given the cases to me now." Tenny was staring at the floor. Her mother leaned over and gave her a big hug and Tenny's tears began to fall. She would always be their baby. Her father grabbed her hands, which were clenched tightly together in her lap. "That's a good thing, Tenny. You'll get him. Your mother and I know that."

It was their third robbery-in-progress call of the day, a typical day in this area. Gang violence and drug-related crimes had erupted in the Los Angeles area several years ago and the police were still just trying to prevent the spread of the dangerous overflow of anger. Today she and her partner had been continuously frustrated by being in the wrong spot at the wrong time.

Not this time.

The silent alarm for a robbery was announced over their police radio as they noticed two young men running across the street in traffic about two blocks north of their location.

"Shit, that's them, Doug! Come on, come on! Go around this traffic!" Ashley reached down and activated the lights and siren. Doug covered the two blocks in seconds, concentrating on traffic as Ashley spotted the suspects running down the sidewalk. The dispatcher was announcing that both suspects were armed with handguns just as Doug made his move, turning the car left into the entrance of an alley to cut off their flight.

"You take the one with the baseball cap," Doug yelled as they both bailed out of the car and drew their weapons.

The next few minutes were pandemonium. Doug screamed commands to the suspects, who were desperately attempting to avoid a collision with him, the police car, or the bus bench which blocked their path around the back of the police car. Ashley spun from the passenger side towards the rear of the car, giving their location and status to Dispatch with her portable radio. Her suspect never even broke stride and hurdled the front of the police car. She whirled back to her left as he took off down the alley.

"Police! Stop or I'll shoot!"

The young man began to slow as he reached inside his jacket and started to swing his torso around towards Ashley. Her world had switched to slow motion the instant she saw him make a move for what she knew had to be his weapon. She sighted in on him with her own semi-automatic. "Get your fucking hands up. Drop it! Drop the fucking gun!" Pulling back slowly on the trigger, all she could see was the revolver coming up and pointing in her direction. At that moment she should have ended it, but something kept her from applying that last ounce of pressure on the trigger.

All she could hear was her heart pounding, unaware that she was still shouting orders. All she could think of was that she had never actually shot at a real person before. How was it going to feel?

Then her world snapped back to normal speed. The kid had dropped the gun on the ground and was running down the alley again. Ashley looked towards Doug, who was taking his suspect into custody. "Mine dropped his weapon in the alley and is running east. Catch us with the car."

The last comment about the car was unnecessary and she knew it. Doug and she had been partners for over a year. They were like Siamese twins. She knew he would recover the other weapon and then pursue in the car.

Ashley took off after the suspect who now had about a fifty-yard start on her. Her 5'5" frame was often described as stocky, but as she burst into pursuit it was apparent that her body was an immaculately maintained endurance machine. This kid was fast, but he would burn out in a few blocks. Ashley just needed to keep him in view and give directions to Doug and the other officers in the area.

The chase went down alleys and directly in front of heavy traffic. The suspect tried to lose Ashley by cutting through some yards. She hated it when they did this. Unless an officer could hear them banging into objects or jumping fences, it was impossible to know if they had discovered a convenient hiding place or were already running through the next yard. This not only complicated a chase, but created a dangerous situation for the pursuing officer. Many cops would have given up as soon as they lost sight of the suspect. Not Ashley.

She searched for more strength and sprinted to close the distance between them. As she entered the yard, she barely caught a glimpse of the kid's hand leaving the rear fence. She ran to the opposite side of the yard to ensure that she wouldn't get any painful surprises on the other side of the fence and started over it. The kid was opening up the distance between them and had made it to the next yard. But from her position on top of the fence Ashley could also see her fellow officer, Clyde, just rounding the corner of the street directly in the suspect's path.

"L-34, he's coming right at you."

She saw Clyde's patrol vehicle come to an abrupt stop and Clyde's huge frame unfold from behind the steering wheel.

"He's made the alley. Here he comes! Hold your position, hold it! He's coming right at you!" Ashley yelled over the radio.

Ashley watched as Clyde stepped to one side of the alley entrance and waited. She was pretty sure that all the poor guy would remember was Clyde's outstretched arm, which looked something like a tree branch and acted as a clothesline.

They had just loaded the now-conscious prisoner into another police car and were congratulating themselves for a job well done when the radio crackled with the Captain's voice.

"L-91, A-8, code two 10-87."

Ashley swallowed her smile and answered with an unmistakeable shake in her voice. "L-91, 10-4, enroute from Mission and Franklin."

"What's this all about?"

"I don't know, Doug, but let's go, I don't want to get in more trouble than I'm already in."

"How could you be in trouble and I'm not? What'd you do?"

"Nothing. I don't think I did anything, but what else would the Captain want from me?"

"I could think of several things," Doug said with a smirk. The Captain had mentioned to several of his peers that he found Ashley extremely attractive.

"Funny. Now let's go. I guess you're booking both prisoners. Serves you right for making me do the hard stuff again."

▼

The Captain watched from his window as Officer Ashley Johnson crossed the street to the Administration Building. She had wild shoulder-length hair which was thick, curly, and a beautiful mix of blond, brown, and auburn. Her white skin was lightly tanned by the hours she spent outside exercising. Yet, the thing that drew him to her was her quick, contagious smile. It made everybody around her want to smile back.

The Captain admired Ashley physically, but it was her raw, natural police instincts that had pressed him to call her. Still a relatively new officer, she already led her fellow officers in apprehended felons. She had the sixth sense. She was good, and he needed someone good. He was caught in the middle of a politically hot case which nobody was willing to admit was being handled improperly. The Chief had demanded that he assign a woman to the case, and she was the department's best. It was time to introduce Ashley to the heart of police work—investigations.

"Ashley, come in. I heard about your arrest out there. Good work. I'm glad you didn't drop that kid."

Ashley had already forgotten how close she had come to killing the suspect. She pulled her gun on suspects all the time, but she had never really had to use it. The odds were against her ever having to use deadly force. It was these percentages that gave Ashley a careless confidence and allowed her to brush off the incident earlier.

The Captain continued, "I called you because I need your help."

Ashley did not respond. He could tell that she was nervous.

"Ashley, the Investigative Division has been working on apprehending a serial rapist that hits only gay women. We've been experiencing communication problems with the victims. Last night we had our fourth attack and the victim just flatly refuses to speak to the assigned investigator."

Ashley was not surprised. The sexual assault investigator, Steve Carson, was a dick. He was a closet gay basher, the worst type of discriminator because he thought of himself as a fair, open-minded person. He truly believed that his disapproval of the gay lifestyle did not show in his work.

Suddenly she realized that the Captain was speaking again, "Go over there right now and see if you can calm the victim down and get a statement."

"I'm sorry, sir. Where is she?"

"She's at the hospital. She got beat up pretty good. She also waited for about two hours before she called a friend who called us. She doesn't have a good history with our department and doesn't think we give a fuck. I don't need to tell you how important it is that we make some progress on this case. So far we've been able to keep this story away from the media, but that's not going to be possible much longer. All we need now is for another minority group to start screaming about how we do our job."

▼

Ashley was excited as she changed into street clothes and drove over to the hospital. This had to be a first. A patrol officer with less than two years on the department getting assigned to a serial investigation. Ashley didn't care that it was because she was a lesbian, which she guessed had been the unspoken reason for her being called in to help. It was the opportunity of a lifetime. She could really make a name for herself now. Hell, if she solved these rapes, she could get a permanent assignment to investigations, maybe even a promotion.

Still drifting through her daydreams of greatness, Ashley walked into the emergency room where the victim was waiting. A nurse directed her to room "A." In an instant, reality transformed Ashley's fantasies into a nightmare. She wanted to turn and run. She had been wrong, she wasn't ready. Not for this. This women was *beaten.* Ashley had seen some badly beaten victims before, but this was different. This woman's eyes were lifeless, trance-like, empty. When she saw Ashley in the doorway, her eyes became defiantly intense at the sight of the great detective who had just strutted in as if she could make a difference.

The true significance of Ashley's job came crashing down upon her broad shoulders. She almost collapsed from its weight. Until now her duties had always been something of a game to her. Piece together a crime scene as fast as you could. Hold it until the investigators arrived. Catch the bad guy if he was around. Never get personally involved. Never stop to think about the lives you entered in moments of crisis. Never take the time to think about the *why.*

Ashley was not just responsible for gathering the pieces this time. She would be the one to come in and put them back together the best she could. At this moment Ashley wasn't sure how to proceed. A variety of emotions were whirling in her head. She wet her lips, opened her mouth to speak and swallowed her heart which had lodged itself in her throat. Tears started to well up in her eyes. She wished that she was with Doug, booking their two dirt-bags.

▼

Margo was tired of standing after spending a long day on her feet in court. So, despite her skirt and heels, she managed to sit down on the courthouse steps in an acceptable, ladylike manner. She must have processed a record number of cases today, though as the years passed, today seemed more like the norm. Margo started to debate in her mind whether there were practical alternatives to this country's current justice system, which seemed to be teetering on the brink of disaster.

"Stop it, or you'll be in a foul mood when Ashley arrives," Margo cautioned herself aloud.

Her mind turned to her lover. Today Margo plea-bargained a sentence for the same man who had brought Ashley into her life sixteen months ago. He had been a petty thief back then. Today he was sentenced to the state penitentiary for armed robbery.

What a great rehabilitation system we have. Margo caught herself drifting back into the philosophical mental diversion and quickly brought her attention back to Ashley. She remembered attempting to deal with the young, aggressive cop who felt her case was sealed tight.

▼

Ashley had argued feverishly with Margo when she discovered that Margo was going to plea-bargain off two of the three charges. The whole time Margo had not only been growing more and more annoyed with the brash young officer, but also noticing how her eyes danced in the heat of battle. When Margo had finally given in and agreed to push for a trial on all three charges, Ashley had unveiled her contagious smile and the deputy DA was hooked.

Margo had managed to spend the lunch breaks with Ashley during the two-day trial. She had found that Ashley slipped easily into discussion about herself. Ashley had been raised by her mother after her father refused to acknowledge the consequences of an affair. Her mother had taught her to be strong and independent. Ashley had never shied away from anybody or any challenge as she grew up. When Ashley was in high school, her mother had dated a cop for a while. Ashley had become convinced that law enforcement was the career for her. She had loved the prestige of the uniform, the respect she imagined from the public, the courage and excitement of all the "war stories." She had worked relentlessly to become an officer and then to become the best.

When the trial ended, Margo had been frantic with indecision. What would be her excuse to see Ashley now? Should she just risk it and ask her out for a casual cup of coffee? Damn, why couldn't she ever really tell if some women were open to propositions from other women?

Margo had still been debating her alternatives as they walked out of the courtroom. Ashley suddenly said, "I wanted to thank you for not ignoring my suggestions about this case. I know that you could have done it your way."

"Why don't you thank me by joining me for dinner?" The words escaped from her before Margo could discipline her thoughts.

It was an awkward and spontaneous proposal which had left both women somewhat shocked. Margo had wanted to become invisible, to apologize, take it back—anything. But all she could do was wait and watch. Ashley had been about to say something else, but Margo's words had seemed to dissolve her own in mid-speech. She looked at Margo and wondered if she had heard what she thought she heard and if it meant what she thought it meant.

Ashley's addicting smile had accompanied her response. "Are you sure you want to get mixed up with a cop?"

Margo's own ego had flared slightly, "I'm not sure I know what you mean." She had tried to give Ashley her best innocent and perplexed look, hoping that Ashley would experience for a moment the embarrassment from which she was still trying to recover.

"Well, I'm looking forward to getting to know all of you. I'll be back in a few minutes. Just got to get out of this thing," said Ashley, tugging on her uniform.

Then she had disappeared, half jogging, half skipping, and seemingly floating down the stairs of the courthouse towards the department. Margo had been left with her heart pounding and her stomach doing flip-flops. Could anyone really be so bold as to say what Margo thought Ashley had just said to her?

▼

Now, as Margo waited, she smiled as she relived the most incommodious moment of her life. Her stomach started doing flip-flops all over again. She had heard Ashley correctly that day and she would never forget that evening.

Margo couldn't remember where they went for dinner or what she ate, but she remembered every other detail of her first evening with Ashley. There had been moments during the dinner when the conversation would break briefly and they would catch each other's eyes. All she had been able to think about was how long she would have to wait to make love to this woman.

The wait had not been long. They had been driving back to Ashley's car and were stopped at a traffic signal. Suddenly Ashley had announced, "If you turn left here we'll be heading in the right direction."

Margo had gotten a lump of lust in her throat. "Your car is back at court."

"My apartment isn't."

▼

Standing in Ashley's personal space, Margo felt as if she was actually up against her. Ashley had instantly created a little piece of heaven when they arrived at her apartment. The lights were dimmed. The perfect song was filling the spaces left void of conversation. She was reaching for Margo.

Her hands landed lightly on Margo's hips. The space became magnetized and they were touching, each woman excited by the other's deep breathing and pounding heart. Margo could feel Ashley's breasts sweep softly across her own and Ashley's grip grow firmer upon her waist. Once again their eyes locked. No smiles. No laughter. No embarrassment.

Ashley leaned into Margo's body and nibbled at her lips. The pounding was no longer only in her heart. Margo's whole body was exploding with passion. She gently grasped the back of Ashley's neck and brought Ashley completely to her in a long absorbing kiss. Ashley responded by backing Margo to the wall and causing Margo's body to fit like a jigsaw puzzle piece against her own. Ashley's movement against her body was unbearable and clothes no longer seemed important. They would disappear as the night continued.

Ashley had one hand caressing Margo's breasts and the other stirring the heat between her legs. She was growing weak against the wall, but Ashley's body held her firmly. Margo could not wait one moment more. She needed this woman now and, through it all, she knew she needed this woman forever.

▼

"Hey, what world are you in, Margo?" One of her coworkers brought her back to the courthouse steps. Margo smiled and hoped that she hadn't been moaning in public.

She wished Ashley would arrive soon. She was about to explode all over again thinking about her. Margo was planning the terribly sinful things she was going to do to Ashley that night when she noticed her approaching.

Margo's passion was replaced by concern. This person walking towards her couldn't be her Ashley. There was no lightness to her step. There was no smile. Where was the joy? Margo had never seen Ashley so fatigued and defeated. What had happened to her gal?

▼

"This guy is not only physically vicious, he tears his victims apart emotionally. The things he says to them—he's trying to get them to give up on their lives." Margo could see Ashley tensing up again. She knew that every muscle in her body was straining to lift the heavy weight thrust upon her today.

"She was his fourth victim and I found out from one of the other detectives that there have been several attacks with the same MO in another jurisdiction up north. They had a rape just two weeks ago." Ashley shoved back from the dinner table and began to pace the kitchen. Margo gave up on Ashley touching her meal. She stood and intercepted her.

Ashley collapsed into Margo's arms, all her tension overcome by fatigue. She allowed herself to relax for a few moments. There was no passion, only stillness. Nothing was said, as if nothing was felt.

Suddenly Ashley stepped back, ready to expend her last reserve of energy. "It's the same thing every time. He always enters the house with either a window smash or a door pry. It's like he thinks he's invincible and doesn't care if they hear him coming. He never carries a weapon and never becomes violent until the victims refuse to make love to him."

"You mean he actually expects them to make love to him?"

"Hell, yes! He spends the first hour or so caressing them, telling them what beautiful women they are, how they don't have to be ashamed of their looks, that they could be with men if they had more confidence in themselves."

"This idiot is sick." Margo was starting to get the whole gut-wrenching truth.

"It gets worse. He talks about the family and how lesbians are responsible for destroying families. He talks about how their own families must be disappointed and how they are contributing to the American family crisis."

Margo could imagine the pain the women suffered because she was seeing it pilfer the happiness and life from her own lover. Ashley had never been so close to such a difficult investigation. Margo knew from her own experience what a toll it would take on her lover. She attempted to steer Ashley away from the emotional turmoil of the investigation and into the facts. "What do you have so far?"

"That's the beauty of this whole thing. We have everything we need to convict this guy, except his identity. He was sloppy in the first attack. We got hair fibers, semen, saliva, even a damn fingerprint from the point of entry. All that means nothing because he's not a known offender."

Margo approached Ashley who was propped against the counter. She slowly leaned towards her and was accepted into Ashley's arms. "You're close, babe. You have a knack for finding the bad guys. You'll get him."

"Well, Steve, the sexual assault investigator, has done a half-ass job so far. He's treating the cases as if they were a series of indecent exposures. The problem is, he just doesn't care about the victims. I'm going to have to avoid him and develop these cases on my own."

Ashley once again stepped away from Margo.

"I know that I'll get him. All I have to do is find the connection that his victims share. He's not just randomly selecting women. He's preying on lesbians and has to have a pretty sure method of identifying them."

"You'll find him."

"I know, but how long will it take?"

3

Steve Carson was gritting his teeth and becoming visibly angry. He had leaned back in his chair with a disinterested stare, his legs and arms crossed. Having finished his first bombardment of verbal attacks on Ashley, the department, and the administration, he seemed to be resting and contemplating his next tactic. The Captain had not expected Steve to take the news of his new partner well, but his hostile protests were a little intimidating even to his ranking officer. After all, Steve was a Paul Bunyan with a badge and gun instead of a blue ox.

He was 6'2", not unusually tall, but his huge frame made him seem 7'0" easily. A massive chest and torso sprouted baby redwoods for legs and arms. His normally sky-blue eyes had turned to steel in their anger. Generally he was thought of as a gentle giant, but not today.

"I don't need a partner, much less some street-soft rookie."

"Well, I feel differently about that." It was actually the Chief's idea, but the Captain was not going to lay the responsibility for this decision on somebody else.

"She has no investigative experience. She'll just get in the way. This is too important for me to take time to train someone."

"She'll bring a type of experience to this investigation that you can't offer, Steve."

"You mean she's queer, too! Great, so she can relate to them, how is that going to help my investigation?"

The Captain tried to alter his approach. "Steve, it's just like any other cultural awareness and sensitivity issue. You have to be familiar with that culture to conduct the best investigation possible."

"Does that mean if all the victims were Black I would get a Black partner because I'm white? You know damn well that wouldn't happen. So in reality this department has chosen to show preferential treatment to a certain class of victim. Is that right?" Steve had manipulated the Captain's logic into a self-serving argument. He had also created a political trap for his Captain, who finally lost his composure.

"Look, Detective, the reason she's coming on board in this investigation is because of your derogatory and offensive attitude toward the victims. You've alienated them to the point that they're barely cooperative and they only provide you with the basic facts. I could care less what you think about these people. The truth is, this idiot who is attacking them is making law enforcement look bad and the investigation is starting to attract state-wide attention. The last thing we need right now is for your own prejudices to interfere with the apprehension of a serial rapist. The only reason you're still on this case is because you're a good sexual assault investigator and we need your expertise."

Steve tried a more reasonable tone of voice. "Captain, you can't tell me you really care if these dykes are getting poked? There are real victims that need our help."

The Captain had never heard Steve speak like this. The harshness was distracting, but Steve's meaning was clear. The Captain didn't want to get the reputation throughout the department of being a gay-lover. His career depended on this investigation just going away quietly.

"Steve, don't jeopardize your career on this case. Just go with the flow and for once be politically smart."

"Oh, so we're not talking police work anymore, we're talking politics."

"You're wrong there, Detective. We are talking police work. We're talking about getting a maniac off the streets."

There was silence for a moment and the Captain decided to throw in the kicker.

"One more thing. It has come to our attention that another department up north has also been investigating attacks with the same MO. We've agreed to work jointly on both investigations. Detective Elizabeth Mendoza will be arriving Monday morning to assist in the investigation of our last attack. Before you start bitching again I'll tell you that she has an incredible reputation throughout the state and that's all I know. Work with them, Steve, or work alone in some other division."

The last word belonged to the Captain and left Steve simmering in anger. Moments later Ashley entered the office. She found Steve sulking in his chair, waiting for any opportunity to win a battle. Her knack for finding trouble had just led her to the Investigative Division.

▼

Ashley had been dreading the inevitable confrontation with Steve all morning as she formalized her transfer from the Patrol Division to the Investigative Division. She knew what an asshole he could be although she also knew that many people liked him, including Doug. Steve was said to be a fair and sensitive person. He often went out of his way to help victims and his fellow officers. But he also had strong beliefs about right and wrong. Ashley concluded that Steve found homosexuality wrong and his opinions revealed themselves in his work. But Doug seemed to think that Steve's bad attitude was more of a defense than a prejudice. He assured Ashley that Steve would overcome whatever it was because being a good cop meant more to him than anything else. This didn't make Ashley feel any better.

When she thought about the victim, though, Ashley no longer cared how Steve felt or what he thought. She was going to get this suspect, with or without his help. Ashley would not allow this one man and his own moral ideals or insecurities to hinder her search for the other man who was viciously imposing his beliefs upon innocent women. She entered the office, primed for battle.

"Hello, I'm—"

Steve vaulted from his chair. "I know who you are and I know why you're here. I don't like it, but that doesn't seem to matter. I don't think you're qualified, but that doesn't seem to matter either. Just stay out of my way. You can handle your friends and that's all."

Damn it! She felt like a damn rookie in the training program again. Steve stormed from the office before she could recover.

It was Friday, but Ashley wasn't ready to go home for the weekend, not even after her confrontation with her new partner. She decided to get on with business and found the files on the prior attacks. She intended to make sure she knew them inside and out. Maybe this guy from up north, Detective Mendoza, would be more amenable to her, although she doubted it.

Ashley sighed to herself, "Welcome to Investigations."

▼

Tenny loved airports because she enjoyed watching people, and airports always attracted the greatest variety, even on a Monday morning. This was a huge airport in a prime location, and Tenny found herself hoping that her ride would be late.

She scanned the family members, boyfriends, girlfriends, and business associates as she walked up the ramp into the waiting room, then looked over the crowd to the surrounding walls where any self-respecting cop would be standing. Sure enough, there was her ride, leaning against the wall. Tenny noted with surprised pleasure that the officer waiting for her was a woman. The sunglasses told Tenny that this was a young officer who still found it necessary to hide the constantly inquiring eyes behind the protection of shades.

Weaving her way through the the throng of welcoming hugs, Tenny began sizing up the officer. She was young and had an easygoing look about her. The relaxed lean against the wall, the simple look of jeans, a red-and-blue rugby shirt, and the easy smile all radiated confidence. Too bad this was only the errand girl. She was much too young to actually be assigned to this investigation.

▼

Ashley didn't know what Detective Mendoza looked like, but she was looking for a Hispanic male. She figured a cop should be relatively easy to pick out of this group of vacationers, families, and businessmen.

"Wow!" Ashley caught herself speaking out loud, but the woman who had appeared from the ramp deserved the exclamation. Ashley found herself admiring the woman with an outright stare.

The woman was Black. No, she was Indian. No, she was South American. She had short, thick, straight, black hair. Her skin was the color of the leather on an oiled and soaped saddle; brown, gold, and tan all thoroughly worn together. She was about 5'7" and slim. Her legs seemed to last forever. She was dressed in jeans and a gray shirt that looked like it came from a set of long johns. A plain black blazer was casually thrown on over the shirt and the sleeves were rolled up. The outfit was completed with a pair of expensive gray boots.

This woman was a magnet for Ashley's eyes.

As the woman drew closer, Ashley discovered her spellbinding eyes. Ashley tried to decide if they were brown or hazel; maybe light brown with a hint of orange. Ashley couldn't find the color to describe them. They were beautiful, mystical, non-revealing. Ashley was still enchanted when a voice knocked her mind back to the present.

"I'm Detective Mendoza," Tenny introduced herself.

Ashley jumped and instantly started to blush. She had been so preoccupied that she didn't even realize the woman she had been admiring was now standing directly in front of her.

"Excuse me." Ashley was struggling to maintain what little composure she had left.

"I'm Detective Mendoza."

"Yes, yes, I'm Offic— I mean, I'm Detective Johnson." Ashley was losing the battle. This woman was unbelievable and she was going to be working with her. Ashley unleashed her disarming smile. Tenny returned a quick, forced smile and started to walk with the flow of passengers towards Baggage Claim.

Ashley fell in beside her. "Why don't you call me Ashley, since we're going to be working together." Tenny stopped.

"How long have you been an officer, Ashley?" Her voice was gentle, but the question seemed severe.

"Over two years."

"Really. And how long have you been a detective?"

Ashley didn't like being questioned like this, not even by this woman. But something about her presence made Ashley answer. "Two days."

"Perfect." Tenny walked away, while Ashley suddenly felt extremely insignificant.

Insignificance quickly evolved into anger. This was the second time in a few days that her partner had had a problem with her level of experience. She had taken it from Steve who had been angry to start with; it was his investigation. This was different. Who did this woman think she was? This detective was a visitor in their jurisdiction. She didn't look much older than Ashley and probably didn't have tons of experience herself, just plenty of attitude. Ashley wasn't about to let her simply walk away.

With a few stretched strides Ashley fell into cadence at Tenny's side. "I don't know what you meant by 'perfect,' but let me make everything clear for you, since you don't know me or my qualifications."

Tenny continued walking. She didn't look at Ashley and quickened her pace gradually to keep this detective off-stride.

Ashley continued, "I got assigned to these cases for two reasons. First, because I'm a good cop. I find the bad guys and I don't lose cases. I've made the most felony arrests in the department in the past two years and I have convictions on all of them. Experience includes more than just years of service."

Still no reaction from the ice-woman next to her. Ashley was having trouble keeping up with her, and Tenny refused to even look at Ashley.

"The second reason is that I'm a lesbian, but that's something we probably have in common." The risk paid off.

Tenny stopped and looked right into Ashley's eyes. Tenny's eyes revealed nothing. No anger. No embarrassment. No defeat. Nothing.

"A risky assumption, Detective Johnson."

"I don't think so, Detective Mendoza." Ashley knew how to play hardball too and held Tenny's look with confidence.

"Tell you what, why don't I go get my luggage and you bring the car up to the passenger loading area. I'll meet you outside and we can try this again." Once again, Tenny turned and walked away.

"I am going to have to break you of that bad habit." Ashley spoke under her breath.

The unmarked police car stuck out like a pink elephant as Tenny watched Ashley weaving through traffic. It was a government-brown sedan with government plates. Tenny wondered what type of department she was going to find herself working with.

She forced the negative thoughts from her head and prepared herself to meet Ashley again with an open mind. The albatross pulled alongside the curb, and Tenny quickly threw her bags in the back seat and slid herself into the front.

"Hello, Ashley, I'm Detective Mendoza, but I hate titles so please call me Tenny."

Ashley smiled and was treated to a genuine half-grin from Tenny. "Tenny, what's that short for?"

"Tenacity, which was how my Sergeant insisted on describing me a few years ago. He began to call me Tenny and it just stuck."

Ashley started to relax. "Sorry for the little scene inside, but you aren't the first person to question my ability."

Tenny looked at her with an intensity that froze Ashley. "Don't ever apologize for doing what's right."

▼

Ashley was uncomfortable with the silence as they crawled through the terminal congestion plaguing the city, heading towards Tenny's hotel. She wanted to get to know the woman next to her but was still feeling somewhat bruised by their airport introduction.

Ashley decided that discussing the investigation would be safe. "I should probably warn you that the actual investigator assigned to rapes is not that pleasant."

There was no reaction from Tenny, not even an acknowledgment that she had heard. Ashley continued, "I was actually brought in because he's been incompetent and the victims have been unwilling to deal with him. My department wants to be sensitive to the victims and thought I could help."

"That's a change." Tenny's sarcasm stung.

"What do you mean by that?"

"Now don't go getting defensive again. You know as well as everybody in this state that your department has been continuously criticized for its lack of sensitivity towards minorities. You guys just don't want to get bashed by the newspapers and community groups again."

Tenny looked over at Ashley who was gripping the steering wheel as if it were Tenny's neck. Tenny quickly changed the topic. "So, the most felony arrests in the department—that's impressive."

Ashley loved to be acknowledged for her police skills and instantly forgot Tenny's stinging comments about her department. "Well, I guess much of it is luck. I always seem to be in the right place. But it really does drive all the guys crazy. They can't understand how a *girl* does it. Of course, police work is my life. I mean I've always wanted to do it and now I want to be the best."

"Being the best means more than having the most arrests." Looking out the window, Tenny winced at having unconsciously launched yet another challenge. She was going to try again to deflect Ashley's attention, but her comment had struck too close this time.

"I don't know what your idea of law enforcement is, but I was taught it's about protecting life and property, and you do that by taking crooks to jail where they belong. That's what our job is, and I do that better than anybody else, including you, probably."

Tenny recognized the rehearsed response of a rookie who still hadn't grasped the complexity of the job. She decided to say nothing.

Ashley couldn't believe the arrogance of this woman. What right did she have to criticize Ashley's department and her work? Now she sat there as if she hadn't heard a thing Ashley had said. Tenny wouldn't even finish what she had started.

After a few moments the silence began to weigh on Ashley again. She decided to give Tenny one more chance.

"I didn't mean to come on so strong, it's just that—"

Tenny cut her off. "Why don't you tell me about yourself?"

Ashley was happy to comply.

▼

When they arrived at the hotel, Tenny thanked her for the ride and confirmed that Ashley would be back later that afternoon to take her to work. With her business taken care of, Tenny turned and walked into the lobby, no "good-bye" or anything.

Ashley headed for the department, wondering why she felt like a teenager with a crush. She tried to convince herself that after a few initial rough spots, they had actually been getting to know one another. However, Ashley forced herself to admit reality. Tenny had not really said anything. She had nodded at appropriate moments, asked all the right questions, and had not shared anything about herself.

Ashley didn't know anything about her. The woman was like a ghost. The image was clear, present, and it seemed possible to reach out and touch it. Yet, the soul was intangible, the presence was slightly intimidating, and if you tried to touch it, the apparition was gone.

4

Steve was seated at his desk, waiting for his two partners to arrive. He had spent the morning distributing all his other cases to different detectives in the division and was now flipping through the lesbian cases to refresh his memory. Now that they had his full attention, he could probably find this asshole in a couple of weeks and get rid of his assistants.

Steve looked over each case and decided that these were definitely hate crimes. The suspect didn't like lesbos. Steve could understand that, he didn't like them either. Shit, women didn't belong doing it with each other. That wasn't normal. It just wasn't natural.

But this guy was sick. Steve wondered what type of guy would have to stick it to a queer in order to feel like a man. The guy must have a severe masculinity problem and can't get any real women, so he has to go rape the dregs of womanhood. Shit, he had to be desperate to rape queers, they all looked more like men than women.

Steve was still flipping through the files as he was developing an informal suspect psychological profile. He reached the end of one file where the photographs were. Looking at the victim, he was surprised when he realized that she was actually normal looking. He remembered interviewing her a few days after the crime and thinking that she was sort of good looking. He never would have picked her out of a crowd as being a dyke.

Steve went back through the files, picking out the photographs of the victims. They sure didn't *look* like lesbians. They were mostly professional, healthy women. So, if he couldn't pick them out (and he knew women), then how was the suspect doing it?

A twinge of anger swept across Steve's chest, grabbing at his heart momentarily. What made these women different? Why did they choose to be with other women? Steve considered himself a liberal, at least for a cop. He really enjoyed working with the various people he encountered. He found the different races interesting and could accept and value their struggles. But they didn't have a choice about their differences. These women did.

Steve wasn't sure whether he was angry at the women for their rejection of men or at the sick shithead that was hunting them. He was confused by the whole issue of homosexuality. Why couldn't people just be normal?

He started out of his office in search of something sweet. As he stepped into the hall he collided with Ashley.

"Shit." Steve stepped back into his office. Reality, in the form of Ashley, followed him back inside with another woman that he didn't recognize, though he had a good idea who she was.

"Steve, this is Tenny. Tenny, Steve." Ashley made the introductions and quickly backed into a corner of the office, safely out of any crossfire.

"Tenny? What type of fucking name is that? Forget it, I don't care. Let's set the ground rules right now, ladies, or whatever you two are."

Ashley, about to spring from her corner after that remark, observed that Tenny had not flinched, withdrawn, or acknowledged his slur in any manner. She decided to stay back and watch how the ice-woman handled this macho maniac.

Steve continued, "I don't need any help with the investigation. You two are here simply to make the victims feel more comfortable. They should be able to relate to you two. So make them feel better however you like. Just don't do it in front of me."

Steve made a move to pass Tenny and go in search of that sweet he really needed now. He assumed she would move to enable him to pass. She didn't. Steve, annoyed that now he was going to have to physically remove her from his path, made the mistake of looking down into her eyes.

Tenny had a gaze that would have frozen an entire squad in its place. He stepped back. There was no other indication from Tenny of what she was thinking or feeling, but Steve had no doubt. When she spoke there was no anger, only a simplicity that clearly indicated that she was speaking to somebody beneath her.

"Your department requested assistance from mine. They seem to think that a joint investigation would be beneficial to both agencies. I was asked to take over my department's cases. Normally I investigate homicides, but due to the skill and viciousness of this suspect my department elected to have me handle the investigation."

Tenny moved to a chair in front of Steve's desk and took a seat. Steve remained standing, an obvious effort to prevent her from continuing to talk down to him. It didn't help.

"I was a special agent for the FBI for several years and still have many connections within that organization. I have more investigative experience than you and your new partner combined. I wasn't selected to work these cases because of my sexual preference, but because I'm the best my department has to offer. I never work with other people and I never close a case without an arrest to go with it."

Tenny changed her tone slightly and now was speaking as if she was the coach of a mediocre team striving to win. "I'm here because I realize that this guy is beyond one good cop. I don't think I need to like you, Steve, to work with you. The only reason I'm willing to work with either one of you is because your department apparently considers you the best. If we're going to catch this idiot, it will take a team of the best. I hope your department has good judgment."

She stood and walked out of the office. Ashley smiled; Tenny had the art of "the last word" down to a science.

Steve snapped, "What are you smiling at?"

"She's good, damn good. You know it, now deal with it."

Steve knew she was good. He had called a friend up north and had gotten the full story on Detective Elizabeth 'Tenacity' Mendoza. Still, he had not expected to feel somewhat intimidated by this woman. She was right about one thing, though. They didn't have to like each other.

▼

The next day the investigators all convened in the meeting room. When Ashley and Tenny arrived, Steve was already seated at the head of the conference table, his case files neatly stacked. Tenny walked past him without a word, took the seat at the other end of the table, and spread her case files in front of her, opening each one. Ashley seated herself exactly midway between the two, again trying to remain neutral and safely out of the line of fire.

Tenny looked up at Steve. He had on an old baseball shirt and a pair of jeans that had been to too many painting parties. He was unarmed and had no other equipment with him. Tenny knew that he was ready to work. The clothes made him comfortable for the day of studying before them.

Ashley was preparing to take notes with a lap-top computer. Tenny took in the high-waisted black skirt, nylons and heels, even a freshly starched shirt buttoned all the way to the top. Ashley had on her weapon, handcuffs, ammunition, and her badge.

Tenny had noticed Ashley's look of surprise that morning when Tenny answered the door wearing an outfit similar to

Steve's. She had even stepped in the room thinking that Tenny wasn't ready. Tenny had let her in and watched as Ashley tried to figure out what to do with herself while Tenny finished getting ready. Tenny was tempted to explain the significance of dressing comfortably when you know that your day will be spent doing nothing but dissecting cases, but instead decided to let Ashley figure it out. Why make her feel like a novice again?

Tenny began, "Steve, let's go over what we have on the suspect, and then start in on the victims."

Steve surrendered none of his nonchalant attitude. "We ain't got nothing on him or the victims, so I guess we can call it a day."

Ashley was not about to put up with more attitude from Steve this time. She had spent the entire night thinking about how to work with these two and solve this serial rapist case. Steve was not going to spoil her efforts or ambitions. "Steve, why don't you grow up. I am not going to try to find some lunatic and baby-sit an overgrown child at the same time."

This got Steve to sit forward and snap, "You! Baby-sit me? Sorry, honey. I'm the one that's been saddled with a inexperienced rookie. No, no, you won't be babysitting, but if you pay close attention you may learn about investigations."

Steve began to spread his folders out and turn to the suspect information page of each report. "I think he's a Caucasian male. At least, none of my victims reported any accent. They said he was well-spoken and didn't use any common street or ethnic slang."

Tenny glanced at Ashley before she also started to turn to the suspect page of her reports. She admired Ashley who had taken her tongue-lashing and was already making notes as Steve spoke. Tenny wondered if Ashley had provoked him on purpose to get him going. She would have done the same.

Steve was continuing, "—at least not bad. The body odor that is reported sounds more like plain male sweat to me, rather than a transient, unkempt, dirty smell."

"You're probably right. It's been hotter than hell this summer." Tenny jumped right into the discussion.

"Yeah, that worries me. I mean, it's over ninety out and this guy is running around in a solid wool ninja suit, complete with a black ski mask taped to his sweater. He's got to be good not to get noticed in that outfit. We know it's wool because we analyzed fiber left behind. We also know that he tapes his mask because unfortunately one of our victims tried to pull the thing off." Steve tossed a photograph the length of the table to Tenny. "That's her; he really did a number on her." Tenny only glanced at the photo. Even after all the homicides that she had investigated, she still avoided whenever possible having to look at the evidence of violence and pain.

Steve finished, "We got some semen too, but that's it besides the general physical description."

Ashley corrected Steve. "Wait, we got a fingerprint and some hair from the first rape scene."

"We did?"

"A fingerprint, you guys got a print? Is it usable? Did you run it through the systems? Where is it?" Tenny's questions were coming in rapid fire, and Steve didn't even have time to be annoyed at the exposure of his lack of thoroughness. He was digging through the files for the first rape case and praying that he had done all the follow-up on the print.

Ashley rescued him immediately. "The print comparison was handled, but there were no hits anywhere."

Steve stopped searching, sat back and took a deep breath. For a moment he had felt like a street rookie who had screwed up a simple task. Had he given these cases so little attention that he didn't even remember something so basic as a damn fingerprint? He could feel the others looking at him. His unprofessionalism humbled and embarrassed him. He vowed not to slack off on this case again; he was too good of a cop to have these two make him look bad.

They spent the remainder of the morning and their lunch hour reviewing the suspect and victim information. They struggled to find a pattern with the victims. Any pattern: age, profession, affiliations, types of vehicles, homes, date of attacks, even hair color. Anything that tied them together.

"Well, we're back where we started. The only thing they all have in common is that they're—" Steve caught himself about to use a common slur. But the slurs didn't seem appropriate anymore after hours of examining the victims more closely with Tenny and Ashley. At least he didn't have to use them in front of his partners and unnecessarily cause more friction than already existed.

Tenny and Ashley exchanged questioning looks as they observed Steve stumble at the end of his sentence and retreat into silence. Ashley decided to rescue him again. "What I don't get is how he's figuring out that his victims are gay."

"We figure that out and we catch the bad guy. Let's look at your tips." Tenny wanted to keep working. They weren't finding any answers, but they were narrowing the scope of the question.

▼

They had divided up the sixty or so tips which the police department had received since the media had been given a short story on the rapes and been provided with the tip-line phone number. Tenny was amazed that Steve was reading the tips for the first time. The reason Ashley had been asked to join the investigation was becoming all too clear. Steve had not even completed the routine follow-up investigation for this series of rapes. He had handled the cases like a burned-out veteran. Steve knew that he would have to work hard to rebuild his credibility.

They had been at it for about two hours in complete silence, each reading a stack of letters. Then Steve began to read out loud in an excited voice. Tenny and Ashley looked up expectantly.

"'Not too many people know this about him, but I do because I have been his mistress for eighteen years. He's a good man and he means well, but he just doesn't know how to relate to women. Except, of course, to me. He's raping women that belong to the other political party in an effort to create a panic. Let me warn you, he won't be easy to take alive. Seeing as how he's the President, maybe you all should arrange to have him assassinated and burn the files which he keeps with the CIA.'"

By this time Steve was finding it impossible to read with a straight face and he finally burst into laughter. Ashley couldn't believe some of the odd tips she had read, but Steve's easily had to be the weirdest. The two of them were enjoying themselves as they maliciously expanded on this woman's proposed theory.

Ashley looked down the table to Tenny. She was smiling that same little half-smile she had revealed at the airport. Maybe she saw the humor, but who could really tell with the ice-woman. Ashley wondered if there was anybody who knew Tenny well enough to know what she thought, how she felt, who she was.

▼

Steve became visibly impatient. As the time drew closer to six, he glanced at his watch or the clock, contributing less and less to the discussion with every passing minute. "Are we done?" Steve asked with a slight tone of annoyance.

"Must have a date," Ashley commented to Tenny, as if to excuse her partner's rudeness.

"That's right, I do, and my mom will kill me if I'm late again," Steve came back in a lighter tone and manner which made Ashley laugh. Her infectious smile smoothly spread to Steve and materialized on his own face. Working with Ashley might not be so bad, he thought. He looked down to Tenny who appeared to have missed the entire exchange and was busily making notes to herself. Steve couldn't understand how such a warm-looking woman could be so cold. But now wasn't the time to ponder personalities.

Steve slid his car keys down the conference desk. "Ms. Tenacity, if you manage to pull yourself away from those cases, feel free to use my company car to get around town this evening. It's on the first row of the unmarks. It's brown."

Tenny smiled as she pictured herself walking through a parking lot full of the standard-issue brown government vehicles, trying the keys in each.

"A smile. The woman must like her freedom." With that, Steve said his goodbyes and was gone.

▼

"What are you planning to do?" Ashley asked Tenny.

"I think I'll work for a little longer and then do some exploring."

"You're welcome to come over for dinner. Margo always makes enough to feed the neighborhood when it's her turn to cook. That way we eat leftovers her other nights and she only has to cook once a week."

Ashley laughed at her lover's sly laziness. But Tenny politely turned down the invitation and went back to working on her notes. Ashley felt as if she had been dismissed. She stood for a moment watching Tenny, wanting to see what Tenny saw, to feel what Tenny was feeling. Ashley had the uncanny sense that this woman solved cases with her mind, heart, and soul.

Ashley said good-night and departed after receiving a "bye" from Tenny, who didn't even look up from her work.

▼

"Come on, babe, let's go out to the deck and relax." Margo loved these long, warm evenings which eventually drew her outside for long walks or just relaxing on her favorite lounge chair.

Margo walked through the French doors leading out to the deck from the dining room and sank into her chair. The twelve years she had spent in the District Attorney's office had finally taught her to stop with the constant work and enjoy her free time, what little she had. As she watched her lover cross the deck and sit on the edge of the spa, she reflected that Ashley was her only hobby. Since Ashley had been in patrol with the odd hours and days off, they normally only got to spend a few hours together each week. Margo cherished that time.

"Ashley, it's so nice to have you working regular hours and home with me."

Ashley smiled. "Well, I'll still have to work weird hours sometimes."

Margo ignored Ashley's reminder and changed the subject. "You know one of your fellow officers got totally sucked in by Dayton today."

"That doesn't surprise me. The only thing that keeps Dayton employed as the Defense is his ability to smear cops." Ashley's own run-ins with the attorney had always left her simmering, although he still had never successfully distracted, confused, or angered her on the stand.

"I saw this poor boy losing his cool and tried to give him the relax sign, but he was already locked in a wrathful stare-down with Dayton. Once again he got just the reaction he was seeking. I think it really hurt our case." Margo noticed that Ashley was not really listening. She was looking off into the distance and didn't even notice that Margo had stopped talking.

Margo decided to change the subject and asked Ashley how her first real day in Investigations had gone.

Ashley's face came to life.

"I can't believe how much there is to learn. I thought I knew it all from being on the streets and involved in so many big arrests. But this is different. It's as if working the streets is a sport and working investigations is an art. It's the details that count." Margo could feel her lover's excitement. "Like today, I couldn't figure out why Steve and Tenny looked so dumpy. I mean they were dressed for a day's work in the yard and not the office. Oh, but sure enough, they knew what they were doing. I was so uncomfortable I could barely concentrate by the afternoon. Pieces of equipment just kept coming off and each time those two would kind of smile at each other."

Ashley couldn't stop. "You know, Steve is better than I thought. You should have seen them testing each other. Of course, it was no contest. Tenny's amazing. It's not so much what she knows, even though it seems like she knows everything; it's more the way she approaches things. She's so thorough and analytical. I would call it absorbing. She doesn't miss a thing.

"Rumors about her are already starting around the division. They say she turned down several opportunities to be promoted in her department. They say she could have been a captain by now. I can't believe it, she looks so young. Margo, wait until you meet her. You'll be hooked, she's so impressive."

"Sounds like you already are." Margo couldn't believe what she was hearing. Sure that Ashley never spoke with such passion about her, she stalked back into the house. Ashley, equally surprised, bounced up to follow her.

"Sweetheart, the woman only fascinates me professionally. Detective Mendoza is a block of ice on a personal level."

She caught Margo at the bedroom door, grabbing her by the waist and spinning them both onto the bed. "Nobody could do for me or with me what you can, babe." Ashley felt like an idiot. How could Margo not know that she was the best thing that had ever happened in Ashley's life, even better than becoming a cop? Margo was so sensitive, so sturdy, so sensible, she was everything Ashley needed. Ashley gently kissed Margo on the cheek. "You are *it* for me."

Margo sighed. She felt plain, average, boring. What did Ashley see in her? Did Ashley still believe, at twenty-three, that making love could solve any problem? Margo, fourteen years older, loved Ashley's youth and innocence, but wondered how she would be able to keep her lover happy for long.

Margo felt as if she shouldn't let the issue pass, but Ashley's tender touch weakened her momentary displeasure. After a few kisses, Tenny Mendoza was the last thing on either mind.

It was a slow morning for TRANS-CAL Airlines, not unusual during the summer months. There weren't as many commuters and those that were forced to fly elected to catch later flights during the lazy summer days. The six o'clock flight this morning had been practically empty. Apparently this had made two of his passengers feel more relaxed and open. It had allowed him to catch them and add two more to his list.

They had been seated at the rear of the aircraft, away from the other passengers, holding hands and being intimate throughout the flight. They didn't even seem embarrassed when he came back to take their drink request. The two women had smiled at him and declined his service, obviously not wishing to be interrupted again.

After the plane landed, he walked out to an empty gate boarding desk. At this hour he had plenty of privacy. He activated the computer and called up the reservations for today's date. He found Flight 368 and entered their seat numbers.

"Got ya!" One of them had made the reservations directly with the airline and the tickets had been mailed to her home address. It was so easy, he had to chuckle to himself.

He took out his little black book which held the names of all the women he had identified as queers. The names included the dates which he entered them. A minimum of six months had to pass before he would select a name. The time was his best protection. The police would eventually start connecting his crimes and search for his pattern. Shit, they were so predictable. But the trail would be hidden by the memories of the victims.

He added this woman's name and as he did so he felt his tension growing. He couldn't believe the arrogance of these women. What they did in their private lives was bad enough, but to bring their sexual perversion out into society and attempt to corrupt others with their behavior was completely unacceptable. His victims were so easy to select. They were the bold, the confident, the comfortable ones. The ones that threw their sickness in the face of decent human beings. They deserved to be taught what real love was all about. They deserved the experience of having something taken away. They had to be stopped before one of them took somebody else's mother away.

He shut down the computer. Close to hyperventilating, he needed some fresh air. He also needed some sleep after the six flights up and down the state last night. He would sleep now. When he awoke, he would start preparing for his next lesson.

T enny was the first to the department the next morning. She enjoyed the freedom that Steve's car gave her. Last night, Tenny could not resist the opportunity to drive by each victim's residence and thoroughly check the areas. Once again she had been unable to find any connection between the victims. Tenny was beginning to feel as if they were dealing with a man not only insane but ingenious. There was more than luck involved in his method of selecting victims, and he had been exceptionally clever at developing his method. Yet, what had kept him in only two jurisdictions? She had checked for similar attacks throughout the state and none existed. When so many cities intermingled at both ends of the state and so many lesbians were scattered all over the place, why weren't the attacks more spread out? She had never seen this pattern before.

Working on a tip, Tenny walked into Steve's office and made a phone call to someone who had reported a prowler. The woman had also said she was being followed.

"Hello, is this Maggie?"

A tired voice on the other end of the line responded that it was.

"Maggie, this is Detective Mendoza from the police department. I'm sorry to call so early this morning, but I need to speak to you before you leave for the day."

The voice was waking up. "That's all right, I'm glad to finally hear from somebody."

Tenny hesitated, then decided on a direct approach. "Maggie, the media hasn't been privileged to this information, but the serial rapist you heard about is only attacking lesbians." She heard Maggie catch her breath. "Oh my God. It really is him. How could he know?"

"My partner and I will be watching you for a few days in order to establish whether in fact somebody is following you," Tenny reassured her.

The voice was awake and alert, "I don't want to be rude, Detective, but I *know* somebody is following me. I've been so scared that for a week now I take somebody with me wherever I go, a friend sleeps over each night, and still I hardly get any sleep."

Tenny decided not to address the anger she heard building in this woman's voice. Excuses for the lack of action on the police department's part would just make her more angry. Instead she stayed on a positive track.

"We will have this person out of your life today in that case. Now what kind of car do you drive, and what type of car is following you?"

▼

Tenny had collected nearly all the necessary information on Maggie's schedule as Steve walked in. She was surprised to see him this early, but he looked fresh and even anxious to get to work. He didn't even scowl at finding Tenny seated behind his desk using his phone.

Tenny hung up and moved so that Steve could sit at his desk. He sat down and looked at the notes she had scratched out.

Steve noticed that Maggie left for work about 6:45 each morning. He looked at his watch. "Guess we're going to get coffee on the road this morning. It'll take us about twenty minutes to get over there. We'll have just enough time for a quick stop if we leave right away. Are you ready?"

Tenny was caught off-guard. Steve was treating her as if they had worked together for years. He knew exactly what needed to be done and knew that he didn't have to confirm or explain plans with her. She guessed that this was his way of trying to regain some of the professionalism he felt that he had lost. She was surprised at how friendly and easygoing he could be.

"I'm right behind you."

Steve scribbled a note to Ashley and they were on their way.

▼

"OK, I didn't enjoy myself last night or get a bit of sleep because this case was bothering me. I'm a good cop and I've worked hard at building that reputation. I know you're a good cop too, and it's important to me what you think."

Looking straight ahead and speaking as if giving a prepared speech, Steve was obviously uncomfortable. Tenny smiled as she imagined him in front of the mirror this morning rehearsing.

Steve continued, "I've been a real asshole lately. Not because of how I feel about homosexuals, but because I've let it affect how I do my job. I'm not normally like that. I can put my personal feelings aside and give this case my best, like I know you'll do. But more importantly, I want you to know that I'll be watching your back. You can trust me to be there whenever the shit hits the fan."

Tenny knew it wasn't that simple. Prejudices were developed over years and could not be laid aside at a moment's notice.

"Thanks, Steve," she said encouragingly. "I know we're all trying to make the best of this improvised team. Knowing that your partner is going to be there when you need help is the most important part of this job. I'm glad I can count on you." She hoped her words would not be put to the test.

▼

Steve pulled to the curb a block away from Maggie's house, just as she was backing out of the driveway.

Tenny instructed, "I have her route and she goes down a few blocks to get to an intersection with a traffic signal. I guess it's difficult to get on the boulevard during the morning commute. She'll actually come back at us and we can pick her up there. Let's give it a few minutes to see if anybody else picks her up right out of the gate."

They waited for almost a minute and no other vehicles even moved. "Got to go if we're going to catch her." Steve put the car into drive and moved away from the curb. They arrived one block over just in time to see Maggie pass. Steve waited for a few cars in heavy traffic and then cut traffic off as he forced his way into it. They followed her to work and watched her park and walk into the building.

"Well, if she is being followed, the guy is better than we are." Steve sounded discouraged.

"Remember that this has supposedly been going on for over a week. The guy has got to have her routine down by now and can pick her up during the day. We need a good place to sit and wait." Tenny was trying to think of a way they could look inconspicuous in this vehicle which almost advertised itself as an undercover police car.

Steve seemed to be reading her mind. "Don't worry, I'm an expert at making my *patrol* car disappear. Of course the easiest thing to do is to get out of it. We can pass as average citizens having coffee in that cafe over there."

They were finishing their third cups of coffee when Steve's eyes focused over Tenny's shoulder.

"Whatcha got?" Tenny didn't turn to look.

"He just made a pass on her car. He's parking down the street from it. He's getting out, get ready to move." Steve noticed that Tenny was still casually sipping her coffee with no hint that this was work and not simply a friendly meeting. She was good.

"He's a white male, twenty to twenty-five, blond with a mustache. He's got on jeans and a white shirt. Shit, he's coming in here."

"We're out of here. He only sees backs. You're too distinctive. He'll remember you if he sees you twice in one day." Tenny was giving orders and already standing with her back to the door as she heard the bells above the door jingle their warning.

Steve quickly stood and partially turned away from the door as he fingered through his wallet for the appropriate bill. "Me?" he said. "Sorry, Miss, but any red-blooded male is going to notice and remember you. Let's just get out of here with as little production as possible."

They left and walked down the street to a pay phone. Tenny called Maggie and asked her if she could run a quick errand so they could confirm that this was the guy who had been following her.

Moments later they were positioned to watch both Maggie and the stalker. When she came out of the building, they could see that he was surprised. He stood up quickly and headed for the door, but stopped just inside.

"She knows him. He doesn't want to risk her seeing him," Tenny spoke softly to herself.

Steve would have never interpreted his actions like that, but he knew that Tenny was right. Subtle, yet obvious. He was going to have to stay on his toes to keep up with this investigator.

Maggie pulled away from the curb and her follower jogged over to his vehicle, got in, and started to trail her. Steve once again allowed some traffic to get between his target and his own vehicle and then cautiously began to track the suspect. "That's a rental," he remarked. "It's almost as obvious as this car." Tenny nodded her head in agreement.

Tenny had told Maggie to go somewhere which would not appear unusual, but to use numerous changes of directions and take about fifteen minutes. Steve was doing an excellent job of staying back.

"Tenny, I think we should take him after she finishes her errand. We have enough for stalking with her two prior reports and the information she gave you over the phone this morning."

"We don't have any threat and that's one of the elements of the stalking law." Tenny had not spoken arrogantly, but something caused Steve to snap.

"So are you suggesting we simply keep following this guy when we know he's up to no good? We can't stand by and wait for it to happen. What are you trying to do, get him on something more?" Steve's voice was betraying his frustration. He knew that Tenny was right, but they couldn't just wait. He had no patience for using people in uncontrolled situations to make cases stronger.

Tenny responded calmly. "Hey, if he is the rapist, then we already know he's not stupid. We need blood, prints, and hair. He's not just going to cooperate with us because he's awed by our authority. You know that doesn't work much these days. We need something good on him, and we need a reason to get into that car."

Steve, frustrated and sarcastic, snapped back, "What do you suggest, since you seem to have all the answers?"

Tenny ignored his tone. "Why don't we try to panic him into doing something stupid. It shouldn't be too hard to burn ourselves in this thing." She patted the dash as if the car was a reliable and trusted steed.

Steve composed himself and smiled. He turned to Tenny. "I think I'm going to be saying this often, but lady, you're good. I like the way you think."

▼

When Maggie arrived at her destination, the suspect pulled to the curb about two hundred feet behind her. Steve passed the stalker's vehicle and Maggie's as she got out. Then he went about a hundred feet further, made a U-turn, and parked, facing the suspect. When Maggie left, Steve barely let the stalker pass before whipping another U-turn with a dramatic screech of the tires, falling in directly behind him.

Steve laughed, "You think he knows he's being followed?" Tenny smiled.

They could see the man checking his rear-view mirror every few seconds, hysteria almost visible on his face. Steve reached down for the police radio's microphone and dramatically brought it up to his face as if speaking into it.

"This should be the final touch."

It was Tenny's turn to be impressed, "Nice thought."

Now panicked, the stalker actually looked over his shoulder and instantly broke off from following Maggie. When the police followed, he took off.

Steve grabbed the red police light and attached it to his dash. He was about to activate the light and siren when Tenny stopped him.

"Wait. Let him violate a vehicle code section first or else we've got nothing."

One block later the stalker went through a stop sign and on came the lights and siren. Tenny used Steve's police radio and informed the dispatch center that they were in an unmarked vehicle and in pursuit.

The stalker drove like a wanted felon as he blew red lights without slowing. He was a good driver, but Steve stayed right with him.

"Is this stupid enough for you?" Steve yelled above the siren.

"I didn't expect such a severe reaction! Where's a damn marked unit so we can drop back?" Tenny hated pursuits, especially in cars that didn't look like police cars. Hell, people barely yielded to fully marked vehicles. Getting them to yield to anything else was simply an amusing wish, but Steve moved smoothly through the traffic.

Finally Tenny saw a marked patrol car coming towards them from the other end of the block. The stalker was trapped between them with no place to go. Tenny slipped off her seatbelt and opened her door an inch or so as Steve was still barrelling down the street.

"What the fuck are you doing? Close the door!"

"No way. We can't let him run. I hate chasing people. I hate running."

Steve was amazed. "Shit, you must be crazy!"

At the last instant the stalker tried to swerve his vehicle through the front lawn of one of the houses. But the Officer in the marked car didn't let up and rammed into him, clipping his rear quarter panel and spinning the stalker's car out of control until it stopped on the grass. Before the stalker could even regain his bearings, Tenny was at his door with her gun in his face. He was taken into custody with no further problems.

The man was placed under arrest for attempting to evade a police vehicle. They discovered that he also had a suspended Arizona driver's license and was wanted in that state.

Steve walked over to Tenny, who was standing near the stalker's vehicle. "The marked unit will transport him back to the department for us." Steve took a dramatic deep breath and loudly announced, "Guess we're going to have to tow this car, can't leave it on this front lawn and can't drive it, not with that rear end messed up so much. Well, better make sure there are no guns or drugs in it." He opened the door and winked at Tenny.

The car was spotless inside, as rentals usually are, and Steve had just about given up after looking through the car. He was bent across the driver's seat in an odd position to look under it when his hand touched something other than the springs he had expected. Steve pulled it out from under the seat.

One look made him sit directly up, banging his head on the steering wheel. Steve fought free from the car as if it were about to explode. Tenny started towards him as he finally negotiated his huge frame out the passenger door. He came around the back of the car and held up what was in his hand. It stopped her dead in her tracks. A black ski mask, with black electrical tape still attached.

▼

Tenny knew it had all been too easy. That the rapist would fall into their laps on the first tip was the type of thing that happened in fairy tales, but seldom in real life. Hope dimmed quickly for the three investigators as they questioned the man they had arrested.

The suspect turned out to be Maggie's brother. The two had been best friends, even as adults. But when Maggie had finally been honest with him about her sexuality, he had severed their relationship. He had realized his own selfishness and prejudice soon after, but never found a way to apologize. Every time he had tried to approach her, he had found himself at a loss for words, frightened that she would reject him as completely as he had rejected her. That's why he had been following her, waiting for the courage. He had fled from the police because he knew he had the outstanding warrant in his home state and didn't want to spend time in jail out here.

Steve stood and walked out of the room without a word.

Ashley, who had joined them back at the department, followed him out to the hall.

Tenny was not sure why they had left, but she was not finished. "Your story is quite believable and we'll find out soon if it is true; Maggie is on her way down here. You better start thinking of the right words to say. However, before you do that, I have some more questions for you."

▼

Steve was able to contain his anger long enough to get into the hall, but then he lost control. He began to curse and kick at the air.

"What's the problem?" Ashley asked, annoyed.

"What's the problem? Don't you see? We spent time running around following this guy who's feeling guilty over nothing."

Ashley had no patience left for Steve's insensitivity. "You think it's all fucking *nothing* when somebody's own family turns on them because of their lifestyle? How do you think it feels to have something that you're supposed to have forever taken away from you by the exact ones that you're supposed to be able to rely on no matter what? What the fuck does family *mean* to you, Steve? It obviously means much more to that poor guy in there!"

Steve was stunned. His own family meant the world to him. Their love was simply taken for granted. But Ashley, fighting her own memories, didn't notice that Steve had already backed down.

"I guess if I'd been your sister you would have abandoned me too. That's right, isn't it? You, like so many other family members, wouldn't try to understand. No, you would just succumb to the societal pressure to pronounce being a queer wrong and turn your hypocritical disgust on your own flesh and blood. It's not right, Steve. Today you have the opportunity to be a part of a family trying to heal itself, but all you can do is throw a temper tantrum like a child because you didn't get to catch your rapist."

Tenny emerged from the interview room in time to catch the last sentence in Ashley's barrage. Steve looked as shaken as the man Tenny had left inside the room. She spoke gently to defuse Ashley's anger. "Ashley, Maggie's here. Can you go get her and bring her down here, please?"

Ashley nodded as the anger began to slide back down inside. She walked away as Tenny turned to Steve.

"Should I bother asking what happened?"

Steve, now embarrassed, did not respond. Tenny could sense that a further confrontation was not what Steve needed.

"I found out some extremely interesting information after you left."

Steve knew that he was about to be professionally shamed again because he had left the room without obtaining all the information there was to gather. He said nothing. He felt everything: confusion, despair, fatigue, guilt, and insecurity. Tenny continued, "Maggie's brother doesn't own that mask and rented the car a week and half ago from the airport when he arrived."

Tenny was bringing the detective in Steve back to the surface, and he identified the next necessary steps. "I'll call Impound and have them move the car to the lab for immediate processing. Then I'll call the airport and get the list of everybody who has rented that car since the rapes began."

"It gets better, Steve. Maggie's brother wasn't the prowler. He adamantly denies it and his shoe size is wrong. I checked the original report with a photo of a print left outside Maggie's window."

The hope was returning to Steve's eyes. "I think we need night surveillance on Maggie's address, what about you?"

"It's 113 Palo Verde Ave. We would be fools if we let this opportunity get by us."

Tenny looked down the hallway. Ashley was leading Maggie towards them. Maggie had a lost, childlike look. Ashley had already told her who had been following her and that he was now waiting to speak with her. Ashley showed Maggie to the door and then gave her hand a gentle squeeze of support before ushering her inside. The three investigators stood outside the room, but no one spoke. Each hoped that Maggie's brother could find the right words.

▼

"I don't know about you two, but today has been too much for me. I'm going to go work out." Steve had plenty of thinking to do. This investigation was messing with his head. In the past he had thought that he had all the answers. Now he wasn't so sure. The two women he was working with *seemed* normal. But he knew they were different. Now that he no longer felt threatened, Steve didn't know what he felt.

As he left, he turned to Ashley and said, "If I ever act like such a jackass again, just shoot me, OK?"

His disguised apology was rewarded with a smile. But Tenny couldn't let his opening pass without a playful remark.

"Guess I'll be back on a homicide investigation tomorrow."

The three of them laughed, and Steve left, feeling forgiven.

Ashley turned to Tenny, "Do you want to work out? We've got a good gym here, or I know great places to run."

"Thanks, but I try to avoid exercise whenever possible. I'll probably be sore from the twenty yards I sprinted during our arrest earlier today."

Ashley laughed. Tenny seemed to be loosening up a bit and Ashley couldn't resist the temptation to get to know this woman better.

"Well, if you don't want to work out, then let's do the second best thing and go eat. I know a great place out on the coast. We can have a beer, kick back, and let the sun put an end to a hard day."

Tenny thought the idea sounded marvelous. "What will your girlfriend think about that?"

Ashley wouldn't let Margo interfere. "She goes out with her work buddies all the time. She won't care."

▼

Steve walked into the weight room and immediately started to feel better. After all, this was his domain and he was undeniably the most intimidating person here. His buddies who usually worked out with him were patrol, administrative, or investigative officers. Best of all, they were all men. Not too many of the women officers ventured into the weight room. For some reason they chose to work out at the public gyms.

"Hey, Steve-boy, how's it going?" Mitch shouted across the room as he spotted his fellow officer. "How do you like working with your new *female* partners?"

"Well, let me put it this way, it's been an eye-opener." Steve didn't really intend for the comment to be taken in a negative way, but his buddies instantly seized it and started to share all the one-liners that came to mind about lesbians and homosexuals in general. Steve went about his workout, not contributing to the dialogue but occasionally laughing so his buddies would know that he was still the same old Steve.

The boys were still doing their comedy act when Doug walked in. There was instant silence. Doug was a man with a reputation. Everybody knew how close he was to Ashley, and he had confronted many other officers about their inappropriate jokes and comments. The boys felt that Doug would snitch them off because of some twisted attraction he had to her.

He noticed the hush sweep across the room, something he had become accustomed to ever since he stopped tolerating the insensitivity that often surrounded him. Doug knew that within fifteen minutes or so the boys would have escaped to some local bar to continue their derogatory remarks, which would then include him.

Sure enough, after twenty minutes Steve and Doug were the only ones left in the room. Doug liked Steve. He was a good cop and he did the job for all the right reasons. "I heard you guys picked up a possible suspect today."

"Yeah, but it turned out to be nothing." Steve remembered Ashley's stinging use of the same word as he said it.

"Well, this one may take time."

"You know, Doug, I thought this investigation would be an easy one. I just assumed that because the victims were all—you know, *different*—that the link between them would be obvious and just point to our suspect." Doug couldn't help noticing Steve's discomfort. "But that's not how it's coming out. I mean the victims are so diverse, it's like they have nothing in common except that they—you know." He couldn't even make eye contact with Doug.

Doug couldn't help laughing. "What did you think, Steve? That because the victims were lesbians, they would all look the same, dress the same, go the same places, have the same backgrounds; that they would all be clones of each other? Come on, Steve, I thought you were more open than that."

"So did I."

"How's Ashley doing?" Doug was curious.

"She mostly tries to stay out of the way. This Tenny gal from up north is basically the boss. She's pretty sharp. I think Ashley will do fine as long as she does what she's told."

Doug got a little defensive. "You know she's pretty bright. She'll probably do fine without being told everything."

"Doug, I didn't mean that she didn't know anything. It's just that this investigation is too important. If she tried to get creative on her own and made a mistake, I think it could cost her her career. Hey, by the way, what is it with her family? I made a comment today about this poor slob we hauled in and she almost took my head off."

"What did you say?"

Steve repeated the whole story about Maggie, her brother, and the confrontation Steve had with Ashley. "She's a little over-sensitive, I guess. It seems like they both are."

"Steve, won't you ever learn? You don't know anything about either of these women. You can't assume that you do." Doug shook his head. This was really going to be a learning experience for Steve.

Ashley put the top down on her little red Mazda and drove to the top of the canyon, working her way west towards the ocean. She wanted to show Tenny the valley, but she noticed how Tenny's attention seemed to be fixed on the fantastic homes nestled against the canyon walls.

"Do you like checking out the different types of houses?"

Tenny only nodded in response.

"Well, then let me show you some of the best." Ashley started to navigate the narrow roads of the hills. Each crest of a hill or turn of a corner seemed to reveal another treasure of residential architecture. Ashley was rattling off details about how the different houses were constructed. Tenny found herself impressed by Ashley's knowledge and started to forget about her own self-imposed walls.

"How do you know so much about these homes?"

"One of Margo's good friends works for a big construction company that does most of the work in these hills."

As they continued, Tenny never took her eyes from the houses and spoke little. Occasionally she would ask Ashley to slow down for a better look at a special design. After a while, Ashley was silent as well. Then Tenny spoke as if she was talking to herself. "If I could do it all again, I'd be an architect, so I could build such beautiful things instead of always having to watch things and people being ripped apart."

Ashley, surprised, looked over to her, but Tenny abruptly turned away.

▼

They arrived at the beach as the sun began to sink through the sky towards its resting place below the ocean's surface. Ashley parked, got out of the car, and was almost to the door of the restaurant before she realized that Tenny wasn't behind her. She turned around and saw Tenny waving to her from the sidewalk. She walked back, more than just a little perplexed.

"What are you doing?"

No response. Tenny just turned and walked across the street. Ashley followed, not wanting to give in to Tenny's arrogance, but curious all the same. They went into the liquor store down the block and Tenny purchased an expensive bottle of chardonnay, a bottle opener, and a package of cheap plastic champagne glasses. Tenny left the store without a word and with Ashley on her heels.

They went back across the street and down to the beach. Tenny walked directly down to the edge of the dry sand and sat herself down. Ashley, speechless at Tenny's spontaneity, sat down beside her. Tenny opened the wine and poured two glasses. She handed one to Ashley and proclaimed, "Best seats in the house."

It was quiet and cool as they watched the waves timidly break and roll onto shore. Ashley broke the silence with a harmless question and was treated to a friendly response from the woman seated next to her.

"I know you don't like to work out, but do you like sports?"

"I love sports, but the only thing I play is football. It's my weakness."

"Really? I love football too. Margo hates it. Who's your favorite pro team?"

Tenny looked at her as if she were crazy. "Who do you think!"

"Yeah, I guess that was a stupid question. You know my idea of a perfect Sunday is to get up early and have coffee while I read the Sunday paper and then hit the couch with Margo and watch some good football."

"I thought you said Margo didn't like football."

"Well, she likes the couch and me. She puts up with the football. If it's a good game, you'll even catch her getting into it. Anyway, she does football for me and I go camping for her."

"You don't like camping?"

"No, I like camping and I love the outdoors. But when Margo goes camping she really enjoys roughing it. She loves backpacking. I guess I'm kind of a wimp, but I'd rather just pitch my tent and kick back."

Tenny laughed. "That sounds kind of rough to me. My idea of camping is going to a first-class resort hotel located in a forest."

They both laughed and Ashley felt as if she might actually be getting to know this woman who still reminded her of a spirit. They joked, laughed, talked, and finally grew hungry enough to relinquish their spot in the sand in search of food.

While they were waiting for dinner, Tenny seized on a pause in the conversation and once again surprised Ashley.

"How long has it been since you spoke to your mom?"

Ashley was caught completely off guard. Instinctively she reached up to a charm that dangled from her neck. "What makes you ask that?"

"Your reaction today with Steve. Maggie's brother seemed to have triggered some of your own pain. I remembered you mentioning to me on our drive from the airport that it was only you and your mom when you were growing up. Plus, the only time you talk about her you use the past tense."

Ashley was amazed that this woman, who seemed so disconnected to anybody, had been sensitive enough to notice something few people knew. She had taken months to confide even in Margo.

"It's been about five years."

Silence. Tenny didn't interrupt this time; she knew Ashley would speak eventually.

"She caught me at home with my first lover. It was an awful scene. Screaming, yelling, crying; so much pain and no way for me to explain or make it better. How do you explain why you're attracted to other women? How do you make people understand?

"My mother crumbled. I don't know if it was disgust or a feeling of failure or what, but she couldn't look at me anymore. She didn't throw me out or try to make me feel like trash. I mean, she wasn't mean or hostile. She just couldn't look at me anymore. I left after a few weeks. She couldn't even say goodbye."

Gently Tenny inquired, "How old were you? Where did you go?"

Ashley looked away from Tenny. "I was eighteen. I had just graduated from high school." She paused. "My mom didn't tell me to leave. She didn't even ask me to leave. She knew I didn't have anywhere to go."

Tenny refrained from pointing out that Ashley's mother had not tried to stop her from leaving.

Ashley finished, "I stayed with my girlfriend for a while. She was twenty and had an apartment which she shared. But that didn't work out either, so when I got a job, I moved into a place of my own. I lived by myself until I finally moved in with Margo."

Ashley was still unconsciously fiddling with the charm. The tears were caught on the edges of her eyes. One blink and they would spill over to her cheeks. As she fought to remain composed, she saw her own pain reflected in Tenny's eyes.

8

He left her in tears, tied gently to the bed. It wasn't concern about her going anywhere that made him tie her, he only needed adequate time to leave the area. The air was fresh and he felt weightless as he stepped out onto the rear porch. Pausing for a moment, he was so satisfied with himself that he started to take his mask off so that he could enjoy a leisurely stroll in the early morning solitude. He had been a wonderful lover tonight, and he felt that he had truly made a difference in the poor woman's life. She hadn't fought him like the one did two weeks ago. This one seemed to be listening to his logic. Her tears were probably for all the years that she had already wasted with other women.

He was removing the tape that held his mask in place when a car came down the street. Not panicked, he simply stepped back into the shadows of the porch. Nobody would ever notice him from the street as he stood surrounded by darkness.

"What the fuck is this?" His calmness vanished as the vehicle turned into the driveway. He recognized the sedan as the girlfriend's, but she was not supposed to be here. He had watched these two for a month and had their pattern down. Why was she here? Now he was trapped. The car's headlights searched the porch as it rolled slowly up the driveway. The lights swept across his figure in the shadows and suddenly the car came to a jerking stop.

He cursed himself, "Run, you piece of shit, you can't afford a confrontation." He jumped off the porch, running down the driveway past the car. Once to the street he turned and started sprinting the six blocks back to his own car, calculating how much escape time he had left. The calmness that he had lost moments ago was beginning to return.

His precise mind figured that it would take the girlfriend a few minutes to recover. Then she would once again panic because she didn't know whether he had actually been inside the house or not. She would go in and take at least a minute to find her girlfriend. Next, the horror of the reality would paralyze her. Her reaction at this point was critical. If she put all the pieces together right away and didn't let her emotions take over, she would be on the phone to 911 by this time.

A siren began to wail in the night. "Shit, she's keeping it together! I screwed up! Shit!" Scolding himself, he kept running as he tried to figure out which direction the siren was coming from and how close it was.

By the time he reached his car, his hands were shaking so badly he could hardly unlock the door. The screaming siren was ringing in his ears, almost upon him. Panic was clouding his mind.

He got the car unlocked and lunged inside. Just as the door shut, lights came around the corner. Diving down on the front seat, he watched and listened as the night was filled with blazing, spinning red and blue light. Then the siren was silenced. The police car had slowed down significantly. The glow of red and blue was extinguished as the officer approached his car. A harsh, brilliant light sliced through the night as the spotlight began to move steadily from one side of the street to the other.

He knew the officer had not seen him because the light had swept twice into his car without hesitating. The officer moved past him and continued down the street. Forcing control, he held his breath and concentrated on the sounds of the night. It was quiet. Since he was quite a distance from the house, he didn't think any other officers would wander this far away for the time being.

After about ten minutes had passed he cautiously sat up. A couple blocks away he could see the glare of a spotlight as the police sealed off the area and prepared to search. He removed his mask and touched the key in the ignition, but then realized that the police would hear his car start. It would act as an alarm in the silence of early morning.

He didn't know what to do. Maybe try to just stay down in the car until the police left. But he felt too close, almost as if he were entangled in a police net. He didn't want to stay. Maybe he should leave the car behind and walk out of the area. But where would he go? It would be getting light soon and he would stand out in his ninja attire.

Then it came to him. Fortunately he was parked facing down a slight incline. Releasing the emergency brake, he slid the car into neutral and held his breath while waiting for the car to move. At first he started to feel the panic spreading through his mind again. The car wasn't moving. Then he noticed that the parking sign which had been near the front of the car was passing by his passenger door. The car was rolling, silently and smoothly, away from the danger.

He coasted half a block down and made the first right turn. He let the vehicle coast as far as possible, then started it and calmly drove away as if nothing had happened. At each intersection he expected to be challenged by a police vehicle, but he encountered none.

The place where he had stashed his change of clothes was not much further, and he was beginning to feel relaxed. He only needed to change his clothes and get rid of the rental car and then he would be safe. He knew that he had been amazingly lucky this time. His overconfidence had almost got him caught.

As his attacks increased in frequency, he would have to be even more careful. Tonight was a frightening reminder. Stupid mistakes had already been made during his first attack and he couldn't afford careless fuck-ups anymore. He knew he wouldn't stop his mission. He couldn't stop.

▼

"I think that we need to expand our neighborhood check. I spoke to the girlfriend and she's sure she would have noticed a car engine starting in the area. She said that she was sort of listening for it because she was afraid that he might come back."

Steve was talking to the sergeant coordinating the field follow-up. Tenny was seated on the victim's back porch next to Steve. Her department had notified them within ten minutes of receiving the 911 call. They had caught the first flight north and managed to arrive within a few hours of the original call. Tenny had gone directly to the hospital and had been with the victim as the rape examination was finished. Steve had responded to the scene to oversee the field investigation and evidence collection. When he was sure that everything was being done properly at the scene, he went to the hospital. Steve found the girlfriend seated in the emergency waiting area. Sitting down next to her, he identified himself, then sat quietly until she wanted to talk.

It was about eight o'clock in the morning when they returned to the scene. Steve had immediately requested that the sergeant assign additional officers to the neighborhood check, since people would be leaving for work soon, and also to expand it out another three blocks. Now Tenny and Steve sat quietly on the porch, each trying to focus on the investigation and forget the emotional and physical brutality of the crime. Both were exhausted. Both were frustrated. Both looked defeated.

"I'm going to go call Ashley to let her know what we have. I'll see if she can settle her court case so she can get up here tonight. I'll get an unmarked car, too, so we can get rid of the patrol car we grabbed earlier."

Tenny stood wearily. Steve watched her scan the surrounding neighborhood, always looking for *something* that everybody else had missed. Tenny started down the driveway and then stopped as an African-American woman approached her. Diane Barker's hair was pressed into the accepted Caucasian look of most female television reporters. It fell like a mane over her shoulders. Her skin had the smoothness of a well-worn stone and the shine of temptation that Tenny's favorite coffee bean had. Her green, cat-like eyes took in every detail. If the presence of this woman hadn't annoyed Tenny so much, she may have even found the reporter attractive.

The other officers in the area suddenly looked busy. None of them were going to deny her access. They didn't want to become the target of her hostile reports. Diane Barker made a living of embarrassing cops. Since this was Tenny's investigation, her fellow officers were happy to let her deal with the reporter.

Before even reaching Tenny, Barker was questioning. "Detective Mendoza, I thought this was a rape scene, what are you doing here?"

Tenny was anxious to escape. "All of your inquiries should be directed to the on-duty press officer. I'll be happy to contact him for you."

Barker was angered by Mendoza's predictable tactic. They had an extensive history of confrontations and Mendoza always managed to keep all her information to herself. "You know I've already talked to him, and I got the packaged response. But he did say this was a rape, so what is a homicide detective doing here?"

Tenny raised her eyebrows and shrugged her shoulders. She stepped past Barker and continued to her car. Barker was not intimidated by this woman who so many treated like a legend. She stayed right on Tenacity's heels.

"I've done some checking; this is the fifth rape in four months. Is there a serial rapist loose? Who's that officer back on the porch? I don't recognize him. I have this victim's name and I want the names of the other ones."

Barker's last demand set Tenny off. "You know you can't have those. If you print this victim's name it will cost you your damn job and your employer millions. Why the hell don't you back off and stay out of my fucking crime scenes or I'll personally take your ass to jail."

As Tenny climbed into her car she instinctively checked the area for that damn television camera but saw none. Barker wasn't sure she really had anything or the camera would have been there. The news viewers wouldn't be treated to Detective Mendoza's temper tonight. Tenny would be sure to have a press officer present in the future.

"I'm not going away," Barker assured her. "I'll figure out what's going on."

Tenny pulled away from the curb, muttering, "That's what worries me." She knew, however, that the confidentiality laws were on her side with rape victims, and she knew that the connection between victims had not been discussed in any of the police reports. Barker would have to be fucking amazing to piece together this puzzle.

Tenny drove to a pay phone and called Ashley's department. While waiting for Ashley to answer her page, Tenny thought about the week she had spent down south. Ashley had spent most of the week setting up a complicated computer grid to enter information on the victims so that they might discover a pattern. Tenny thought this was a useless waste of time, but since she really didn't know that much about computers, she let Ashley go ahead. Tenny didn't want to pass up any chance to catch this rapist.

Steve had spent the week going back through five years' worth of hate crimes against gays and lesbians, searching for a possible suspect. A few possibilities were quickly eliminated by

Steve as they provided solid alibis. Meanwhile, Tenny talked to the victims and their friends, searching for a link. The days ran directly into the nights because all three wanted to be involved in surveillance on Maggie's house.

They worked the surveillance in four-hour blocks with another detective assigned by Steve's department. Although they knew the next hit would be up north (if the suspect stuck to his pattern), they couldn't be sure that the suspect would not prowl at Maggie's again in preparation for a future attack. This was their best chance.

The pay phone rang and for a moment Tenny forgot it was for her. She looked around as if somebody else might be waiting for a call. Then she came completely out of her dreamlike analysis of their investigation and lifted the phone from the receiver.

"Tenny here."

"Tenny, it's Ashley. How's the victim?" Ashley's concern was evident in her tone.

"Like all the rest."

"Shit, did we get anything more on this asshole?"

"Not yet. We're just finishing up a neighborhood check, but it doesn't look hopeful. The victim's girlfriend came home early from work and surprised the prick as he was leaving. All she could provide was that he was fast and in that damn ninja suit. Is Margo going to get your case continued so you can get up here?"

Ashley had been stuck behind on a burglary case which was scheduled to go to trial. Ashley's frustration filtered across the long-distance wires. "The stupid defense attorney, Dayton, doesn't like me and convinced the judge not to go for a continuance."

"Can't Margo plead it out?"

"No, he won't take a plea. He's been trying to crush me on the stand ever since I hit the scene, and he thinks this is the case which will do it. Margo's got a couple of fast ones up her sleeve, though. I should be able to get out of here the day after tomorrow."

"Great. Has your wonderful computer program solved our investigation yet?"

Ashley laughed, knowing that Tenny had no appreciation for the magical products of modern technology. "Is this woman against machine?"

"No, I've learned to work with them as long as somebody else is around to tell them what to do. I've got to get back to the scene. Try your best to get up here. I want to handle all the follow-up ourselves on this one, so bring your little carry computer with you."

"It's called a laptop."

"Yeah, well bring it. Hey, one more thing. Try to get your department to kick up the surveillance on Maggie's to twenty-four hours."

They both knew that she could be the next victim, but convincing the administrators to dedicate more staffing to a *maybe* could be impossible. "I'll do my best. See ya."

"Yeah." Ashley heard Tenny hang up.

▼

The Officer was halfway through his last block on the neighborhood check. This was a recently refurbished area that had been stolen from the lower classes and rebuilt by young professional couples with money to burn. These people had worked hard to rid their neighborhood of poverty and crime. Moving the poor out and building over their memories, they now felt secure in their homes, and it seemed that they rarely paid attention to what was happening in the neighborhood. After all, practically all the houses and cars had alarms, the streets were quiet, and everybody that lived there was just like them. They had nothing to worry about.

He hadn't had any luck so far and was starting to consider this a waste of time. The detectives were stretching this whole thing out because they were desperate. They had little to go on in this case and the police were starting to look bad. He wanted to catch this rapist too, but the chances of finding a witness or evidence this far away from the scene seemed slim.

The Officer walked up to the next front door and knocked. A man in his thirties, wearing an expensive suit and still carrying his briefcase, answered the door. "Excuse me sir, we are checking with all the neighbors in this area because early this morning a young woman was raped in her home a couple of blocks away."

The man looked astonished at first, but the look quickly changed to a look of fear. The Officer noticed the change and knew he had just stumbled onto something.

"Oh God, are you sure? I can't believe it. I knew I should have called the police."

The Officer ignored the man's question and focused on his last statement. This man had seen something and the Officer wanted to know what. "Why should you have called us, sir? Did you see something?"

The man stepped past the Officer and walked down the path to the sidewalk. He looked up and down the street, then said something that made the Officer want to arrest him for stupidity.

"The sirens woke me up. I looked out my bedroom window just in time to see a person dressed all in black trying to get into a car parked there across the street." The man pointed to an empty parking space.

"I could have sworn the person had a black hood on, too, and I thought that was suspicious, so I came downstairs to get a better look. I heard the police car go by as I put my robe on and walked down. When I got to my front porch, the person I had seen was gone, but the car was still there. I assumed that the police car had frightened him away, so I walked across the street and got the license number."

The Officer tried to hide his disgust. "What was the license number?"

"I wrote it down inside. I'll go get it." The man ran back inside the house.

The Officer couldn't believe what he had heard. What did it take for people to call the police? Sure, they called whenever they were inconvenienced with loud noise, illegally parked cars, or a theft of some type. But when they were witnessing a crime or something suspicious, they rarely notified the police. The Officer was relatively new but he had already heard all the excuses for not calling. The few times that citizens actually reported the suspicious things they saw, the police usually made great felony arrests. Early this morning could have been one of those arrests.

The man came back with a napkin which had the license number written on it. At least he had done that much. The Officer thanked him. He didn't ask the man why he hadn't called or tell him that the suspect was most likely hiding in the vehicle while he was copying down the plate. The Officer didn't know how to educate the man without letting his disgust show. He simply got the man's name, address, and phone number and started to leave.

"I'm sorry I didn't call." The man looked like a child who knew that he had done something wrong and wanted somebody to tell him it was all right.

"So am I." The Officer left. He walked back to his car, reached Tenny on the police radio, and gave her the plate. He didn't give her all the details. Her day was going badly enough already.

▼

Tenny was yelling at Steve from the end of the driveway. "Let's go, guy, we got something." Her voice no longer sounded exhausted; this time there was excitement.

Steve ran down the driveway and as he reached Tenny her face broke into a genuine grin. This was the first effortless smile he had seen from this woman, and it was as magical as her eyes.

"We got a plate on the suspect vehicle. I already checked it out, it's another rental. Let's go, I got us an unmarked."

Tenny turned and started to jog down the street. Steve followed, but he didn't see an unmarked anywhere.

"Where's the car?"

"Right here, get in." Tenny was jumping into the driver's seat of a clean, maroon Jeep Cherokee.

Steve got in and in total disbelief asked, "I thought you said you got an unmarked. What's this, your car?"

"Steve, not all police departments drive dinosaurs. We don't like being picked out as cops by the car we drive."

Steve looked at all the toys in the car, including a mobile phone, and was momentarily impressed before refocusing his attention on their mission. "What makes you think this lead is going to go anywhere? Why are you so excited? When I did the follow-up on the rental Maggie's brother was driving, it was a dead end. The suspect provided all false information when he rented it. What makes you think it'll be different this time?"

Steve didn't diminish Tenny's enthusiasm. "Steve, this is much more than we had five minutes ago. It's something. Even if it's a dead end, it's a trend at last. The guy is using rentals to get around. Shit, it's something."

"You're right. Let's go get this bastard."

▼

The suspect vehicle had been rented from a large rental agency's local office on the peninsula. Tenny used the car phone to call the agency as they drove down the highway. They discovered that the car had been rented yesterday morning and had not been returned yet. Their excitement grew as Tenny shifted to the police radio and alerted her dispatch center that the suspect car was still outstanding. She knew that within minutes every cop in the area would be looking for the vehicle as her dispatchers spread the word to other local police departments. Tenny got back on the phone and asked the agency to have the rental agreement and the agent that performed the transaction ready for them when they arrived.

Tenny's heart was racing. It could all be coming to an end. A sharp local cop would discover the car soon and maybe the suspect with it. The nightmare would be over. She looked at Steve and knew that he was hoping for the same thing. He was wringing his hands with impatience. They were so close.

▼

"Here's the rental agreement." The agent handed the papers to Steve, who passed them to Tenny. She had already alerted her department so that computer checks could be done and gave Dispatch the name and driver's license number.

"I rented the car yesterday morning to a gentleman in his thirties. He acted a little weird, but everything checked out."

Steve wrote down the agent's description of the renter, along with the telephone number listed on the rental agreement. The computer check revealed that the renter lived nearby and a cross-directory check of the phone number verified the address. Tenny and Steve thanked the agent and rushed out of the office.

Within ten minutes they were standing at the renter's front door while two local uniformed officers knocked. When a man matching the agent's description came to the door, Tenny stepped past the officers and took control.

"Hello, Mr. Channing. I'm Detective Mendoza. I'm investigating a rape which occurred last night, and I need your assistance. The car you rented yesterday was apparently used in the crime. I would just like to sort things out with you."

Steve found himself admiring Tenny's style once again. Most cops, including him, would have started out in an accusatory manner. After all, this guy was possibly their suspect. His physical build, at least, matched the description given by the victims. Yet, they didn't have enough for an arrest and a search warrant would take too long. Tenny was helping the suspect build a defense, but if he was their guy any lie would be easily uncovered. That wasn't important now. She was leading him to believe that they really didn't suspect him, trying to put him at ease so that they could get inside his home.

"Do you mind if we come in for a few minutes to figure out what happened?" A moment of hesitation, and then Mr. Channing stepped back. The instant they stepped through the door their eyes began combing the house for any clues, any hints, anything.

Mr. Channing was already explaining frantically to Tenny. "Some little old guy asked me to rent the car for him. He said that he always has difficulty renting cars because of his age, like medical insurance you know. Nobody wants to trust old people with anything. I felt bad for the guy, plus he gave me fifty in cash for my help." As he told his story the man realized that it sounded fictional. Had he really been so easily deceived by a smooth approach and a fifty-dollar bill?

Steve's question revealed his own disbelief. "Where were you last night?"

"I was here with my wife and kid all night. She's at work right now, but you can call her."

Tenny and Steve realized that this guy was telling the truth. His confusion and trembling were real. Both investigators knew they had hit a dead end again. Worse, this time the asshole had set them up by using a third party who would be identified as a possible suspect because of his build. The real suspect was challenging them. He was bold. He was arrogant. He was still out there.

▼

Tenny and Steve didn't speak as they drove back. The rental car had been abandoned about three miles from the attack. With its recovery, the last chance for the good guys had vanished. Of course, they had the vehicle and could process it for trace evidence, but they had all the physical evidence they needed. It was nothing without the identity of this maniac.

Steve finally spoke as they pulled into the department's lot. "I need a drink and so do you. I'm buying and you're escorting."

"Steve, what I really need is a damn break in this case. Something, anything, but I know I won't find it at a local bar."

Determination was the only tone in her voice. Tenny parked, got out, and started towards the building. Steve didn't like what he was seeing. He knew her reputation and that her diligence was often effective, but they had been at this for about fifteen hours straight and nothing she could do would solve this case today.

He caught up to her and gently took her by the arm, which instantly tensed. He knew that he would have to choose his words carefully to avoid a flaring of her temper. "Tenny, whatever you think needs to be done now can wait. If you push yourself too hard, then he'll be winning because you won't be as sharp. You can't let him get the upper hand emotionally."

Tenny looked back at Steve and relaxed her arm. For a moment she looked as if she was about to cry. Steve felt the ice melting. Taking Tenny's other arm, Steve turned her squarely to him and looked into her eyes.

"We will get him." he said, "Not today and probably not tomorrow, but we will get him."

Tenny broke away, thankful for his strength but embarrassed by her need. She turned and walked back towards the parking lot. Steve didn't follow. If she was going to walk away from him, he was not going to make it easy.

Tenny turned back. "Come on, ya big lug. You owe me a drink and lunch."

"Lunch? I think that was just a drink. Where did lunch come from?"

"It's payback for everything I've taught you."

Steve laughed. "OK. I can't argue with that, and besides I will be the envy of all the other guys with you at my table."

"Yeah, and half the women in this town," Tenny added cockily.

▼

The restaurant was crowded with summer tourists. A recommendation would be the only thing to attract so many people to this little hole-in-the-wall dining spot. It didn't sit on any of the main streets and certainly didn't offer any kind of exotic or intriguing atmosphere. The main attraction, excellent pasta, was all that was needed to create the fifty-minute wait.

After a few minutes a woman emerged from the kitchen, caught sight of Tenny, and grabbed her in a hug which the best NFL running back could not have avoided.

"Tenny, where have you been? It's been weeks since Sarah and I saw you."

"I've been working."

"Of course, what else would you be doing? Let me get you a table and tell Sarah that you're here."

After another greeting by Sarah, who was the chef, Steve and Tenny were seated. Sarah had personally taken their orders and sent over two bottles of Tenny's favorite beer before she hurried off back to the kitchen.

Steve was impressed. "My, my, am I in the company of a celebrity?"

"No, I was their first customer when they opened this place together. I was also their only customer that night. They started thinking that the whole world knew they were lesbians and therefore nobody would come to the restaurant. I spent the entire evening talking them out of closing permanently. Now they always treat me as if I own part of the place."

"Well, you apparently gave them good advice. This place must do great."

"It does now; the community saved it. The gay community spread the word about this place. First just among the women, then the men started finding it. Not long after that, the word spread to the local hotels. That's all it took." Tenny sipped her beer.

Steve theorized, "The stomach is the great equalizer among all minorities. Doesn't matter who makes it, if the food is good, then people come."

Tenny laughed. She had never thought about it like that, but Steve was right. Food was often the first barrier broken down between cultures. These days you could walk into any type of ethnic restaurant and find a variety of people represented. It was so easy when it came to the stomach, but enormously difficult when it came to the mind.

▼

Lunch had been marvelous and both of the investigators were leaning back in their seats, finishing off their beer. The conversation during their meal had been light, mostly focusing on Steve's career and aspirations. Although Tenny had enjoyed listening to Steve, she was still turning the case over in her mind and eventually brought the conversation back to it.

Tenny worried, "That woman harassing me at the scene is a reporter. She's trouble, and she's already picked you out as a stranger, so stay away from her. I'll have the press officer give her something on the serial aspect, like you guys did, but that's all she gets. Hopefully nobody will make the connection between the attacks in two jurisdictions. That's why it's important that you and Ashley stay away from this woman."

Steve seemed unconcerned. "I'll be happy to stay away, but you know sex crimes are more difficult for the media to work because they don't have access to the victims."

Thinking of her prior experiences with Barker, Tenny snapped, "Look, she's dangerous, and I don't want her screwing with this investigation."

They sat quietly for a few moments while Tenny calmed down. "You know Steve, there are two patterns which are emerging."

Steve didn't hesitate to allow the conversation to turn back to their case. "One is the use of rental cars and the other is that he is alternating between our two cities."

"Right, what do you think?"

Steve thought for a moment. "I'm damn glad we have surveillance on Maggie's house. That's really our only hope unless somebody tips us off. The rental cars are a dead end. If he's been smart enough so far to use a clean third party, why would he change now?"

Making a fist with one hand and speaking through clenched teeth, Steve continued, "I hate not knowing how he's doing it. I feel like he's got the upper hand and I don't like it! What links our victims when they live at opposite ends of the state? Shit, it could be anything. But the attacks are happening so frequently that there must be something linking them right now."

Tenny leaned forward, her look suddenly lethal. "He doesn't know that we've figured out that he's been prowling at Maggie's. I know it's him, I can feel it in my soul. The luck in this case is about to turn."

Tenny again relaxed. She had been asking herself for quite a while why the luck kept falling on the bad guy's side. It didn't make sense to her. They'd been so close a few times and the luck had gone against them. Tenny knew that a large amount of fate was going to be involved in finding this guy. He was not a simple opportunist, as Steve was implying. His crimes were so well thought-out that only the unexpected was going to trip him up. Tenny hoped their surveillance on 113 Palo Verde Ave. would be that unplanned event.

▼

"You know, Steve, I have to make a confession before you leave." Tenny had pulled into the semi-circular drive of Steve's hotel. "When I went to call Ashley, I also checked up on you from this morning to make sure that you weren't being an asshole to the victim's girlfriend."

Steve didn't appear surprised, but he did seem a little intimidated. It was as if he was waiting to hear the score on his sergeant's exam.

Tenny continued, "She said that you were extremely supportive. She mentioned that you two even discussed relationships and how partners always feel responsible for each other and that it's a good thing to care like that, but to remember that it was in no way her fault. She seemed to feel much better after talking with you."

Steve continued to stare out the window as he spoke. "You know, Tenny, it was like talking to anybody. I put myself in her place and asked what would I feel like and what would I want to hear from a complete stranger. Then I said it. I'm not saying I understand any better why women want to be with other women. But a relationship is a relationship, no matter who it's between. I only made it all right for her to feel something."

"You did a good thing, Steve."

Steve opened the car door and got out, but before walking away he leaned down to the window and for a moment said nothing. His eyes focused on his vacant seat and he began to gently nod his head. Tenny could only guess at the thoughts racing through his mind. She now knew that Steve had the same obsession about knowing the truth and why things happened that she had. He was having a difficult time figuring out the *whys* and *hows* of homosexuality.

Finally Steve concluded his internal debate. "It felt good," he said.

9

"Let's go, guy, we've got a date."

Steve looked up from his work and caught a glimpse of Tenny striding past the office door. Quickly locking his gun in a desk drawer, he dashed out of the office. He saw Tenny heading into the hallway. Steve caught up to her at the front doors to the police department and followed her outside.

"So, you going to pay me back that lunch?"

"No, this is better."

"Better than a free meal? I don't believe you."

They walked past the employees' parking lot and went into the police lot. Steve had a feeling that the day wasn't over yet. "The unmarked, huh? Feels like whatever we're doing, it's business."

"Get in, and I'll explain on the way." Tenny started the engine. Steve stood outside the passenger door, wondering if he should call it a day. After all, wherever they were going couldn't be dangerous. Tenny wasn't armed and hadn't asked him to bring a weapon. Whatever she was up to, she could handle it herself. As if Tenny had been reading his mind, she started to back slowly from the parking space. Steve's curiosity got the better of him and they were on their way.

"Thought maybe you were going to stand me up for a steak."

"The idea never even entered my mind," Steve had a deceptive smile on his face.

"Well, since you've been so good as to join me, I guess I can tell you what's up. I've been trying to figure out a way to get more information about this case out to the community without turning the whole investigation into a media circus. Right now that Barker woman and the rest of the media hounds are only slightly interested, but if they knew what actually linked the victims they'd be out of control."

Steve was a little confused. "OK, what does that have to do with tonight?"

"Actually, this whole thing is your fault. The other day when we were having lunch at Sarah's restaurant and talking about how the gay and lesbian community had really started the place going, it got me thinking about something.

"We really have a strong sense of family in the homosexual community. We've got all different types of people. Different ages, different professions, different religions, different economic classes, different races, different backgrounds. Yet with all those differences we still must act as one to promote our well-being and the education of the masses."

Steve interrupted, "That's me, right?"

"I said masses, not asses." Tenny was laughing before she could get the whole playful insult out, and Steve joined her laughter.

"Anyway, my dear sweet partner, I thought that with all the community's resources available we would be much better off with them involved. Plus, we owe it to everybody to at least let them know what's going on. So I got some flyers printed up and got some friends to start distributing them hand-to-hand so the media wouldn't find out."

"I don't know, Tenny, I thought you were worried about how resourceful this Barker woman is. She'll find out about this meeting if she's really working this story."

Tenny grinned mischievously, "Don't worry about Barker. I took care of her."

Steve didn't say anything for the rest of the drive. He was worried about not being accepted by this community and was wondering if Tenny had made the right decision by bringing him along. He wished that Ashley was there for more support, but she wouldn't arrive until tomorrow.

▼

"We're late, so I am going to take advantage of my authority for once and park in this gas station. Parking around here is impossible, I'll explain it to the attendant." Tenny got out and removed her badge as she approached the attendant. Their conversation was short and she came back and said everything was set. Steve had to smile. Occasionally, the job did have a few small benefits.

"We decided to use the church because we had no idea how many people would show up. It's a huge place. I doubt it'll be full." Tenny completed her sentence as they entered the doors. From the foyer they could see that the church was full, standing room only, in fact.

A woman approached to greet them. "What a turnout, huh? The upstairs is just as crowded. I'm seeing faces I've never seen before, and I thought I had seen them all. The microphone is set up for you, Tenny."

Tenny moved off into the church, leaving Steve standing in the foyer. Steve had never seen such a turnout for these types of meetings. These people came together on short notice to see how they could help, not to complain about the police or interrogate them on the progress which was being made. Tenny had shown him the flyer on their way over. It had asked simply for the community to unite and start working together to catch this guy. Steve stood there amazed. The entire church quieted as Tenny reached the microphone.

Tenny was almost as touched as Steve. She had expected some support, but this was overwhelming. She took several deep breaths to steady her heart and voice before she began to speak.

"I want to thank you all for coming. Judging by your reaction to my flyer, the maniac we're searching for is in big trouble." Her comment got a wave of applause and shouts.

▼

Tenny discussed the joint investigation and its progress so far. In addition, she asked everybody to cooperate in keeping the investigation out of the news, emphasizing that media attention was exactly the type of thing this idiot was looking to attract. Finally, Tenny had also given some suggestions as to how everybody could improve their own personal safety. She was wrapping up. "We are here tonight because the police need your help. We don't have enough eyes and ears to find the suspect. We have to wait to track him by the mistakes he has made and will make again. But maybe all of you could find him by working together and watching out for each other. If there is a stranger who seems out of place in one of our many hangouts, call the cops. If somebody who has no need to know is asking you personal questions which seem inappropriate, call the cops. When something or somebody just doesn't seem right, call the cops. Yeah, you'll increase that poor beat cop's work, but they all want to catch this guy too, and they won't mind a good tip. Trust yourself, instincts are often better than we give them credit for.

"Now before we take questions, let me introduce my partner. He's trying hard to make all of us feel at ease when we have to deal with him and I hope you all will do the same. In case you haven't figured it out, he's the huge guy in back and his name is Detective Carson and he wants to answer all your questions." Tenny motioned for Steve to come down and he started fielding questions before he even made it to the microphone.

Somebody burst out, "Why should we trust the cops? They've never exactly been our friends."

Steve hesitated, hoping Tenny would jump in. No such luck. He was on his own. Thinking back to his own attitude, he realized that in this room only the truth would be effective.

"I'm not your friend, and no cop is paid to be a friend. We're paid to provide protection and serve the public equally. Don't forget cops are humans too. When we're treated poorly and with hostility, then we sometimes aren't that friendly. The more you treat cops like your enemy, the more we become your enemy. If you never try to trust us, then we'll never be able to help." He looked over to Tenny who nodded her approval. Steve added in the silence, "Or learn."

▼

Tenny left about a half hour later when all the questions had been answered. Several people had stayed to talk with them, but Tenny became icy and slid away as soon as possible without being rude. On the other hand, Steve was finding the people in the room fascinating and had insisted on staying, saying he would catch a cab to his hotel. Steve had spoken with all types of women and men who had approached him to say nothing but thanks for his work and his honesty. They seemed so anxious to give him a chance, Steve felt he owed them the same opportunity.

▼

Tenny was still sorting through her emotions as she drove home. This meeting had been so powerful and moving. She had caught herself on the edge of tears several times. What moved Tenny the most was the number of women who were there that had not "come out" before but were doing so now because *their* community was facing a serious threat. The threat of AIDS received their emotional and financial support but had not forced many of them from their silence. This threat to women could not be addressed with money. If people didn't stop lying to friends, family, and society, how could others start to recognize the stereotypes for what they were: a fiction? Most people didn't even recognize that their daughter, best friend, or boss was gay. How could everybody else not act like it was a shameful sin, when so many lesbians were themselves ashamed of who they were?

▼

Diane Barker threw her overnight bag on the stiff hotel bed. She had been confident that she would be able to obtain some more information from Steve's department. A talkative cop had provided Diane with Steve's name and told her that he was a sexual assault investigator.

She had immediately flown down here expecting to catch this department off-guard. Instead, everybody seemed to be expecting her. Nobody would talk, and the only information she could get from them was what the law entitled her to: the times and dates of any rapes that the department investigated within whatever time period she requested. That information was useless.

Diane sat on the edge of the bed and stared at the wall. There was a serial rapist out there, she knew it. Why else would two departments at opposite ends of the state be working together? But she wasn't making any progress with her story and the station wouldn't work on this much longer.

Diane flopped back onto the bed. "Damn this Tenacity woman." Something told Diane that she was the reason that Diane wasn't getting to the bottom of this story. "Well, she's met her match this time. I'm not going away."

The sun was a fluorescent orange as it began to sink in the sky. This was Margo's favorite time during the long summer days. She grabbed the lounge chair, let her mind settle, and welcomed the night. The sun appeared to crack like an egg, oozing orange and red into the smog that covered the city. Finally a thin layer of pink rose to the top, as if too pure to mix with the dirtiness. Soon she noticed lights igniting all across the valley. Although she was only two blocks up from the noise, dirt, and hustle of the city, Margo always felt miles away from it all.

Ashley was upstairs packing for her trip tomorrow to join the other two investigators. She had almost lost her mind with impatience. Ashley had spoken of nothing but the joint investigation since her transfer. Margo sensed that she was careful not to talk about that other woman detective too much.

She recalled the other night when Ashley had come home late and crawled into bed with the smell of alcohol radiating from her. Margo had innocently asked Ashley where she had been. "Out to dinner with a friend," she'd said. Then Ashley had rolled over and gone to sleep. Though Margo knew that Ashley had been with that Tenny woman, Ashley's distance in bed was what kept her awake well into the early morning.

Ashley had always cuddled up next to Margo before. What had changed that, she wondered.

Margo was trying not to let any jealousy show. After all, she really had nothing to be jealous about. Ashley had never strayed, in fact she hadn't even seemed interested, until now. But just because Ashley seemed interested in Tenny, that didn't mean that they were going to end up in bed together. It didn't mean that Ashley didn't love her anymore. It wasn't anything to get all worked up over.

Margo wanted a serious commitment from Ashley. They had been together about a year and a half. Margo owned the house by herself. They had separate bank accounts, car loans, credit, and even separate closets. They didn't even wear rings. Margo had never worked up enough nerve to buy one. None of this had bothered Margo until now. Margo wanted a piece of forever and she wanted it with Ashley. Close to tears, she sat quietly on the deck as darkness drew in around her. Nothing had changed between Ashley and herself, Margo remembered. At least not yet.

▼

While Ashley packed she thought about how Dayton had purposely dragged out the trial. He had taken an entire day just to select the jury, and with each passing moment Ashley had become increasingly angry. This attorney was being a jerk. He wouldn't accept that Ashley was as good as her reputation and reports indicated. Dayton was convinced that all cops were dirty and that the more arrests they made, the more corrupt they had to be. Ashley tossed her duffel bag to the floor as she mentally threw Dayton from her thoughts. She began to focus once again on the investigation. She hated that Steve and Tenny were working the latest case without her assistance, and she couldn't wait to get involved again. Tenny had been keeping her up to date with a couple of telephone calls a day, but it wasn't the same as being there. Ashley was also eager to be in

Tenny's company again. She had never met somebody so hard to get to know.

Ashley started down the stairs and suddenly she thought about leaving Margo. She was already missing the comfortable feeling that she always had around Margo. They fit together in and out of bed. They understood each other and complemented each other's strengths. They were equals and their respect for each other strengthened their love.

"Hey, gal, what are you doing sitting out here in the dark?"

"I was thinking about you going away." Margo didn't tell Ashley that she meant the possibility of her going away permanently.

Ashley walked over to the lounge chair, sat down in front of Margo, and leaned back until Margo's chest became her cushion. They sat there together, contemplating tomorrow in silence. Finally Margo spoke up in a tentative voice.

"Ashley, don't you think it's time that we made some type of commitment to each other?"

Ashley turned towards Margo and gently kissed her throat. "Babe, I would love to go upstairs and show you my commitment."

Margo pushed her away. "Look, Ashley, you can't do this every time."

"Do what?" Ashley was becoming defensive.

"Every time we have a problem or I try to talk to you about us, you try to avoid a discussion by getting us into bed."

This time Ashley sounded hurt. "I thought you liked making love to me."

"Ashley, you know that's not the problem. I don't even know if there *is* a problem. I just think there should be something more between us. We need to share more than space and sex. I want to share everything with you, honey. I want us to have some goals together. Something to work towards."

Ashley was facing out towards the city. Margo reached out and gently grasped her lover's chin, turning Ashley's face back towards her own. "Look, honey, I love you, that's all. I'm sorry if I upset you." She gave Ashley a long, lustful kiss and soon Ashley was herself again.

"I want you to be extra careful while I'm gone. Don't sit out here like this by yourself. I know it's hot, but keep the downstairs windows shut and please keep my off-duty weapon under the pillow. This creep has got me on edge."

"I'll be careful, don't worry. You be careful, too. Remember, I'm not the one trying to hunt this maniac down."

Brushing Margo's hair aside, Ashley let her hand trail down behind her lover's ear, down her neck, across her chest, and under her blouse, finally coming to rest on her breast. While she gently kneaded Margo's nipple until it rose to hardness, Ashley nibbled at Margo's lips. Although Margo had really wanted to talk to Ashley, her body was already reacting to her touch. She knew that in Ashley's mind any problem was solved, but suddenly the words and Margo's last hour's worth of thoughts didn't seem important anymore. Tomorrow would bring more questions, but right at the moment all of Margo's answers were on the lips of her lover and she didn't want to miss a thing.

▼

He was starting to feel less uneasy. A few days of terminal duty had brought back his usual sense of security. Ever since the near miss up north his heart had been fluttering from anxiety. To avoid his normal routine of flying up and down the state, he developed a feigned ear infection which would keep him out of the sky for about a week. This would give him time to gather his mental strength and settle his nerves. After all, he didn't need to travel right now. He was almost prepared for the bitch on Palo Verde. She was going to be next.

The line of pre-boarding passengers was growing and he glanced up to see how far behind he was. Halfway down the line crowded with bodies and luggage, he saw a woman that stood quietly as if she were the only one in the terminal. She had confidence emanating from her. Something in his gut told him that she was one of them.

He kept snatching glances at the woman as she waited her turn in line. As she handed him her ticket with a polite smile, he noticed it. Proudly displayed around her neck was a charm. Two axes back to back and bound together. It was a symbol of unity among women. Women as warriors, standing together against their enemies. He had seen it before many years ago.

▼

His mother's friend had always been so nice to him. She was at his home practically every day after school. Together they had often filled the late afternoon with games and laughter while his mother had rested because she was often sick. Then one day he had come home and neither his mother or her friend were there. He never saw them again. After a few weeks, his father had stopped making up lies about where his mother had gone and told him the truth. She had run away with her friend who was a lesbian. He hadn't even known what the word "lesbian" meant at the time, but he came to understand. Then he would remember all the moments he had seen his mother and her friend together holding hands and whispering urgently about something. With each memory came more anger—more hate.

▼

The next passenger's impatient voice yanked him away from his obsession. He watched the dyke walk away and decided she would be his next target. He wanted to hurt this woman, strip her of her confidence. No matter who she was or where she came from.

▼
.

Ashley had been casually admiring the airline attendant as she inched her way forward in the line. He was handsome with a gentle quality as he assisted the passengers ahead of her. Yet as she stepped to the counter, Ashley suddenly felt uncomfortable. He was staring at her pendant and his manner momentarily seemed menacing. He looked up from her axes and returned her smile. Ashley ignored her gut instinct.

He took her ticket and started punching her information into the computer without ever taking his eyes off her. "Ashley. That's a delicate name for an obviously capable woman." Ashley didn't respond, she was trying to decide if the comment had been meant as a compliment.

"Hey, you work for the city. My best friend works there too. Which department are you in?"

Ashley had never been shy about her profession and didn't hesitate to answer honestly. "I'm a police officer."

He looked fascinated and impressed. "Whoa, that must make your boyfriend feel secure."

"Don't have one of those." Ashley responded and sealed it with a smile. He handed her the boarding pass and she turned and found a seat off away from the crowd, chuckling to herself.

▼

He finished with the last passenger and thought about the woman, Ashley. For once, this was an opportunity to get to know the dyke he would conquer. He felt playful as he approached Ashley to gain some more insight, which eventually he'd use against her.

"I've got exactly three minutes and thirty-six seconds to get to know you and convince you to go out with me."

Ashley's experience and good judgment should have told her to brush him off at this point. But he was so handsome and she was flattered. She allowed him to continue in his pursuit, and he turned out to be a master at the game. He asked her unusual questions, yet was careful not to get too personal. His voice was hypnotic and his eyes were like a pendulum. Ashley was sure that any straight woman would take him home in a second. For some reason that thought frightened her.

After several minutes, a boarding announcement was made. "Well, that's your flight. How did I do?"

"You have a creative approach, and if a woman could fit you into her life, I'm sure she would." Ashley stood as she tried to let him down gracefully, already feeling guilty for letting this game go on at all. One last smile which was returned without embarrassment and Ashley boarded her plane.

▼

Her brushoff had been expected. In fact, it had been desired. He was now satisfied that this woman needed his lesson. She would be the best victim yet. Strong people make the best victims. He could not wait, she would be worth the risk. He was good and the police were slow. No closer to stopping him. The fact that this woman was herself a cop didn't bother him. It excited him. He went back to the computer and checked her purchasing information. The only information listed was her name. Of course, the police department's address was listed, but this didn't discourage him. He knew how he would find her.

Tenny rolled over and looked at the clock, hoping that the time would motivate her to get out of bed. But time seemed to stand still this morning. Time, the great healer, the motivator, the carrier of new things, was highly overrated in Tenny's opinion. She still thought about her ex-lover each day, even knowing that the feelings were no longer mutual.

Their relationship had seemed inevitable but had been challenged too many times. Tenny had spent many mornings attempting to make sense of two people's love unraveling not because there wasn't enough love, but because there was too much. Why couldn't somebody make love understandable?

Although Tenny had been with other women in the last two years, she couldn't bring herself to trust anyone. The talks, the walks, the sex, all felt like a performance. Tenny had stopped seeing other women about six months ago.

This morning she tried to will herself back to sleep, but as soon as she closed her eyes, the good times came flooding back. Instead of forcing them away as usual, Tenny let them come.

▼

The hotel was just a short walk back from the restaurant, but neither woman was anxious to get there. They took each small trail branching off the main path to the rocky bluffs above the bay, away from prying eyes. Every movement was charged with boundless energy. Everywhere they looked was perfect and beautiful. Every word they spoke was magical and uninhibited. Every time they touched, it was cherished.

Tenny had been captured by her innocence and her experience, her smile and her passionate gaze. That night when they made love, Tenny finally understood the difference between making love and having sex. It wasn't the touch, the feeling, or the act itself. The difference was in the surrender, the release of her body, her mind, and the thoughts that created her soul. Surely this love would never be broken.

▼

"Shit, I can't believe the crap that my mind makes up. Forever, right, that's why she's laying here beside me now. Come on, Mendoza, join the real world and get your ass out of bed." Tenny threw back the covers and flung her memories to the floor with them. She just wanted to be left alone.

▼

There had been silence ever since the forced polite conversation at the airport. Ashley could tell that something was wrong. She had been looking forward to seeing Tenny again and could not stand the quiet which was only broken by the police radio in the car.

"Is everything all right with the investigation?"

"Sure, if you consider getting nowhere all right." Tenny's reply came out sharper than she had intended, but she didn't know how to apologize to Ashley without explaining her mood.

Ashley was determined to get Tenny to talk to her. "What's going on? You seem as if something's wrong."

Tenny continued to look straight ahead. "I woke up in a philosophical mood this morning and my reflections on life have managed to depress me thoroughly."

"I think I know what you mean. Margo is like that, too. She starts thinking about all the problems that the world is facing and she's never satisfied with letting go until she comes up with the solutions. But then her solutions are always so simple, and she knows that for some reason the easy answers are always ignored. Eventually she ends up in a complete funk. So what's got *your* mind spinning?"

Tenny hesitated. "It started with my personal life and ended up with what always puts me into a mood—the job. I'm having trouble finding the motivation to do what we do. Sometimes I think what we do for society has lost its meaning."

Ashley wished she could ask about Tenny's personal life. "What we do still means something to me," she said encouragingly.

"Ashley, are you still proud to be a police officer? No, really, think about it before you answer. We've always been able to stand behind the badge. We say that we're there to protect and serve. But now, thanks to the cops you see on television and in the movies, not to mention the newspapers, when we arrive many people don't know if they're better or worse off. We've been struggling for years to wade through the muck and sludge of society. But there's so much violence and prejudice these days, we get pulled down by it, too."

Ashley couldn't believe how disillusioned Tenny sounded. "Sounds like you don't think too much of your fellow police officers," she snapped.

"That's not it. Ashley, don't fall into the trap of looking at everything through the eyes of a cop."

"That's who I am."

"You're more than that. If you don't use all of yourself in this job, then you'll become part of the problem. You'll slide until you feel like it's *us* versus *them*. That's when a good cop starts to go bad." Tenny continued with more emphasis, "We start to feel as if nobody cares about the fact that we risk our lives and our mental health to help others. Then we either get out of the profession or fight back against a society that doesn't care. Slowly it becomes a battle of *us* and *them* and it's as if nobody sees it happening."

"Hey, there are plenty of good cops out there that just get their job done, and nobody is the worse for it."

They came to a stoplight and Tenny looked into Ashley's eyes. "If you only go out there and get the job done, then you're part of the problem. What we do is more than a job. Why isn't it all right among cops to really want to help people?"

Ashley had never really thought about helping. Police work was a job to her, an exciting and challenging job. Then she remembered what she'd felt in the emergency room when she saw the rape victim. She remembered pulling back on the trigger while the robbery suspect turned, but not firing. She had almost ended somebody's life.

Tenny's voice brought Ashley back to their conversation. "Law enforcement can't endure all the negativity much longer. We need some radical changes. If nothing happens soon, the good cops will start to give up and leave."

"So what are you planning on doing about it, Tenny? You can't give up. You care too much. Your conscience won't let you just sit back and watch. I know you'll find a way to make things right for yourself and probably many of us. That's the type of person you are."

"How do you know what type of person I am?"

"Because, lady, it's in your heart, it's in your soul, and it's shining in your eyes right now. Even when your logic is telling you to give up, your conscience is preparing you to heal. You may feel lost for now, but you'll find yourself. When you do, you'll accomplish things that you thought would never be done."

Ashley reached over and touched Tenny's hand which was resting on the gearshift. Tenny didn't respond. She was slumped in the seat with a worn-out look on her face. But her jaw was clenched, and determination burned in her eyes.

▼

"Let me tell you, Steve, when Tenny and I were in the Academy together, we hated each other. Of course, we were always competing for all the top honors. God, did she piss me off. Still does, most of the time." Frederick had introduced himself to Steve while he waited for his partners to arrive.

"I know what you mean," Steve nodded.

"After we got out of the training program, they stuck us on the same damn squad. Every day we had adjoining beats and every day we had to try and outperform each other by getting the biggest arrest. Of course, it didn't take long to figure out that the job of patrol cop couldn't be done safely with a Lone Ranger attitude."

Steve snickered. "You mean she saved your ass?"

"Yeah, how'd you know?"

"That's usually the only way that women cops ever really prove themselves to their male counterparts." Frederick, impressed by Steve's observation, got strangely intense.

"Well, now we value, trust, and depend on each other. She stuck by me when my career took a turn for the worse a few years ago. My high ethics and standards got me into some deep shit with some of my co-workers who I blew the whistle on. Suddenly I was no longer the high-flying Black cop, instead I was the black sheep. My professionalism was a threat to the 'good ole boy' system. But Tenny backed me up through the entire ordeal. Thank God the rest of the department eventually caught up to our standards, then presto, I made Sergeant."

Tenny and Ashley walked in as Frederick was finishing his story. "Hey, girl, I got a stack of messages for you from the reporter." Frederick held them out as Tenny passed. She grabbed them, threw them in the trash, and headed for her office without saying a word.

"What's with her?" Steve asked, nodding towards Tenny's office.

"She woke up with the world's weight heavy on her mind, and it's taking her some time to shake it off," said Ashley. "Let's give her a few minutes. You can show me the best place for coffee around here and bring me up-to-date with what's been going on."

Steve and Ashley excused themselves and started to leave when Frederick spoke. "Everybody's behind you two. We want you to catch this asshole and take care of our gal Tenny. She's a special person. Ask if you need anything." Ashley and Steve thanked him and walked to a coffeehouse around the corner.

"Tenny has quite a following around this city," Steve observed. "Ashley, you wouldn't believe how people respond to her. They trust her and respect her, but I don't think anybody really knows her. It's kind of like team spirit. What is it that really brings people together for one cause? Well, when Tenny walks in, it's like she's that spirit. It's weird, I can't explain it. I wish you could have been around last week."

"I know what you mean," said Ashley. "But what about you? I think that I'm starting to see the real Steve. Relaxed, friendly, sensitive…."

"You mean not a prejudiced, hypocritical, uninformed asshole, right?" Steve laughed. "Let's just say it's hard to remain close-minded when all the stereotypes you always used in your defense keep getting disproved."

Ashley leaned forward across the table with a mischievous smile and whispered, "You mean you're becoming a liberal."

"Don't push it. I still don't understand why women choose

other women over men. Is it because they've just never been with a man?"

Ashley pushed back from Steve, the smile instantly gone. "You sound like the asshole we're looking for."

Steve didn't like being compared to that desperate wimp and his temper flared. "Well maybe if you gave men a chance you would realize what you're missing."

"I'm not missing anything, and I haven't made any mistake in my life when it comes to who I choose to love. Plus, there are plenty of lesbians who have slept with men out of love and out of experimentation, but in the end they always come back to women." Ashley tried to hold back her anger, wanting to educate instead of accuse. It was the only way to end the hate.

"Look, Steve, if you're asking me why I prefer women, then I can't really tell you. Believe me, I have tried to explain it to others plenty of times. It's more than who I like to have sex with. I don't hate men. I'm not afraid of men. I'm not trying to be a man. It's none of those things." Ashley paused and touched her charm. She needed to make Steve understand.

"It's as natural as all the emotions and sexual drives you feel, Steve. It feels good and right to me, so that must make it normal. Yet when I am intimate with men, I feel forced and constricted. Feeling like that isn't natural. Nobody should have to feel that way."

Ashley could see that Steve was trying hard. He didn't say anything for several moments. She decided to try another approach.

"Steve, why don't you tell me why you prefer women?"

"I don't know, that's just the way it is. The way it's supposed to be." Steve knew there was more to it than that, although he didn't think he could put it into words. Maybe such intense emotions and instincts didn't belong in words.

He sat back and looked at Ashley as if seeing her for the first time. "I think I see your point."

When they returned to the office, Tenny was on the phone. "Hold on, Jim, my partners just came back from coffee without a cup for me. Let me put you on the speaker phone." She turned to Steve and Ashley.

"I asked Jim to do some computer work for me. He's an old friend at the Bureau and can access more computer systems than we could ever imagine."

The voice from the telephone speaker cut Tenny off. "Mendoza, shut up for a second, I think I got something." The three detectives sat straight up. "All of your victims do have something in common, although it was like finding my damn contact lens in a rain puddle."

"Stop dramatizing and tell us." Tenny was impatient.

The voice on the telephone grew quiet as if spreading a secret. "Every single one of your victims had Sallie Mae college loans."

"College loans," Steve repeated out loud as the reality of the obscure connection sunk in. Ashley was already ripping open the victims' files to see where they all went to college or if they had even asked that question.

"Plus, all your victims went to college in California."

Steve grabbed the telephone book and flipped through the pages wondering how a federal college loan agency would be listed.

"There's only one office in the state," said Jim. He gave the location of the office and wished them luck.

▼

They planned their strategy as they drove, agreeing that Tenny would deal with the manager and be the politician of the group. She would be sure to smooth any ruffled feathers. Her role would be the most important since they were going without any type of search warrant. They would have to depend solely upon the cooperation of the office manager.

Steve would handle the records detailing the male employees' sick leave and other absences. Ashley would get the basic information on all of them, go to the local police department, and run them out in the state and national computer systems.

As they drove into town, Tenny summarized their plan of action. "This must be a common link between people, with all the universities in this state and all the people that can't afford them without help. I'm sure that if we were to link any victims together, at least fifty percent would have this in common. But this is all we have, so it's worth treating as if it were already confirmed as our connection. Therefore, the most important thing is that we don't tip this piece of shit off. He's been smart and probably thinks that he's unbeatable. He's been playing with us, now it's our turn. We have to put on the performance of our lives. When we leave, we've got to have the whole place convinced that we were simply three overzealous cops that came here, didn't do a thorough job and left with nothing. The whole time we're there we act as if our investigation is going nowhere and that we're stumped. If we do find a possible suspect, we want him to think we missed him. If this guy is as good as we think, we won't find enough to hook him on today and we don't want to scare him off."

"Don't worry, Tenny, we've got him now."

Tenny corrected, "No, Steve, we don't have him until he's doing time for consecutive felony sentences. Then, and only then, do we have him."

It took Tenny about twenty minutes to convince the office manager to cooperate. There was no need to threaten her with a search warrant or imply that she would be interfering with a serious felony investigation. They had simply talked about the crimes and the information that had brought the detectives to her office. Tenny had carefully explained the legal technicalities and the manager's legal liabilities. Appalled that one of her male employees might be responsible, the office manager opened her office and records to the detectives.

Heading back several hours later, they compared their discoveries. "I think that we have two decent candidates," said Steve, trying to translate his own notes. "The first is a guy that Ashley found who has a criminal history for assault as a young adult."

"But Steve, he's in his late forties now." Ashley was skeptical.

"Hey, both Tenny and I got a look at this guy. He looks great and he fits the general physical. We have no idea how old this prick is."

"You're right, and I tried to keep an open mind also, so I sent a request to the reporting agency for the assault report. It's in the archives, though, and it will take a few days for them to dig it out and send it. Plus, I went ahead and called the federal personnel records and finally got somebody to release his blood type. It's a match."

Tenny erupted, "You did what?"

Ashley, expecting to be congratulated, was speechless. Steve rushed to her defense.

"Ashley, we probably should have discussed this, but those records have to be subpoenaed or obtained under a search warrant. They're protected by an employee's right to privacy."

"What do you mean? You looked at their records at the office."

"But he didn't go into their personnel records. We could have got the blood types there." Tenny's voice was still harsh.

"Ease up, Tenny. She made a mistake that lots of cops would have made." Steve resumed his role as a teacher. "Ashley, the difference is that I was looking only at administrative records where there's no expectation of privacy. It's different whenever you are dealing with blood samples or types. The safe rule is, always get a warrant."

Ashley struggled to defend herself. "I don't need a warrant to draw blood from a felon. This is a felony investigation, and I didn't force anybody to give me the information."

"The difference is, you have a suspect under arrest based on probable cause, if you know what that is." Tenny's sarcasm stung. "Here you have nothing to base any suspicion on any one of the guys that work there and therefore no probable cause," Tenny snapped. "We don't know if the men at this office are the only ones that handle loan papers for all California participants. The files could go other places, too. We don't have anything solid to allow us to dig deeper into any of these guys' private lives. Damn it, Ashley, you're not playing cops and robbers anymore. You need to slow down and think. "

Ashley could barely restrain her temper. "We *know* one of these guys is doing it."

"Look," said Steve. "What's done is done. If it comes up later in a motion to suppress, we can deal with it then. The blood type is common, and at this point in the investigation, it's not critical. I don't think this will hurt our case in the long run."

Tenny was silent, and Steve went on, "Now, the other guy was sick on days surrounding twenty percent of the hits and on vacation during one. Plus, the office is centrally located. If he had to, he could drive to either city that day, hit, and drive back in time to be at work."

Ashley volunteered, "No criminal history on this one, not even a speeding ticket. The blood is also a match."

"It's not unusual for serial criminals to have no other criminal history. They avoid any type of contact with the police. Their survival depends on it." Tenny made an effort to calm down.

Steve interjected, "OK, gang, that's enough, let's concentrate on what we're going to do now. Do we want to let the locals in on this so that we can have surveillance on these two while we eliminate other possibilities?"

Tenny turned to Steve, "Well, do you think we left there with everybody thinking we had totally wasted our time?"

"I think I make a great dumb jock type. No comment from either one of you." Steve lifted a fist in mock warning. "But all the same, I would feel much better if somebody was watching these two. I would never be able to live with myself if there was another hit and we hadn't taken the chance because we were worried about burning ourselves."

"I'm with Steve. Our first duty is to protect, even if it does mean screwing up our case." Ashley looked relieved.

"You don't have to convince me," said Tenny. "Even if we do end up spooking the suspect, the pieces will start to fit together as soon as we figure out the right person. Plus, the local detectives are good, I don't think they'll blow it." Tenny took a deep breath. "We're close. We have tons of work to do tomorrow, but if we get an early start on the phones we may have our man by the end of the day. We'll have to use all the back doors to find out locations during attacks and verify alibis. The one thing we don't want is for this guy to run. He would just disappear for a few years and then resurface somewhere thousands of miles from here and start again. This guy is *not* to slip through our fingers because we weren't patient." Ashley knew that Tenny's emphasis was meant for her.

▼

When they got to the hotel Steve held Ashley's bags while she went to check in. Tenny hung around to say goodnight to her partners. A few minutes later, Ashley stormed up to them.

"I don't know who screwed up, but they say they don't have a reservation for me. Plus, some shit about it being the height of tourist season and some convention, so they can't even give me a room. They called a couple of other hotels and it's the same story."

With a boyish grin, Steve offered, "You can sleep in my bed." He was simultaneously punched from both sides.

Tenny knew that she would have to offer her home as a place for Ashley to stay. She didn't really want to. Nobody had stayed in her home for such a long time.

"Ashley, you can stay with me. I have two bedrooms and plenty of space." The words came out naturally, although Tenny's stomach was tied up in knots.

▼

Tenny pointed Ashley towards the living room. "Make yourself comfortable. I'm going to mix myself a cool drink, would you like one?"

"Sure, whatever you're having."

"Cranberry and pink grapefruit juice mixed together."

"Sounds great."

As Tenny disappeared into the kitchen, Ashley took two steps down into the living room and into Tenny's life.

The room was a mix of black, white, and gray, serious but not depressing. Ashley felt herself relax in the open space with its large windows. On one side of the room, a bay seat invited her to a hypnotic view, while a black-and-white photograph took up the entire opposite wall. Ashley turned up the ceiling lights for a better look.

Bleak and dirty, the scene could have been any alley in America. Seated against the cold gray wall was a middle-aged Black woman, her hair just starting to gray. She wore a tattered hat and a heavy, torn coat. In her eyes were anger, hurt, courage, and knowledge. Down her cheek rolled a silent tear. Each arm was wrapped around a small girl. One looked about three, the other was older. They both huddled in closely, frightened of what tomorrow would hold. This was not the dream they had been promised. Beneath the photograph was a poem.

It starts with an old Black woman seated on the ground,
She has nowhere to go and little help can be found.
Her children are hungry and cold,
The woman cries; she is so tired of being bold.

I wonder how this woman came to be so poor.
Was it her fault or did society just shut the door?
But as she sobs, it really doesn't matter to me,
My heart is ripping and tearing at the scene I see.

Suddenly I realize that my society is not what I thought.
This woman's world is sad and lonely and happiness can't be bought.

I will not send my cash to help her from the ground,
But to this scene, my life and my work will be bound.
I shed my tears as a tribute to this fine woman's dream.
I will not work for her, she is stronger than it may seem.

But every chance I get in my life,
I will attempt to take from the children's future such strife.
It will not happen soon, for I am still new.
But I will help and change life, if only for a few.

Elizabeth Mendoza

The telephone rang, startling Ashley. She walked to the fireplace mantel which was crowded with books: *Of Mice And Men*, *Don Quixote de la Mancha*, and *I Know Why the Caged Bird Sings*. Ashley took one off the shelf and held it reverently. The cover was faded and the book's spine cracked. When she opened it, the pages creaked with age. They were yellowed and brittle. Ashley felt as if she was holding a piece of history in her hands. She figured that these books were probably first editions.

Ashley wanted to discover more. She called out to Tenny that she wanted to check out the upstairs. Tenny, still on the telephone, gave no response, so Ashley boldly took that as permission.

Moving up the stairs, she was mesmerized by a group of three photographs that resembled the one in the living room. Each depicted part of a food line for the homeless that stretched upward along the stairs but never reached the place where food was delivered. Just people, all ages and races, waiting for their small share. They would never truly reach their dreams, not even the simple ones. Ashley remembered driving by real-life scenes like this without even being thankful for what she had.

Tenny's room shared the view with the living room. Unlike the rest of the house, it was full of color, light, and happiness. Fresh flowers were everywhere, and children played in the painting above the bed. Smiles, laughter, the freedom to dream. Tenny lived with hope, too.

Ashley walked across the room towards the window and the deck. As she passed the cabinet against the wall, she noticed a photograph of a woman and a small girl. Their smiles were enchanting. A piece of Tenny's past, Ashley guessed, and a part of Tenny's sorrow. Feeling like an intruder, she turned to leave. Tenny was standing at the door.

"I've made numerous mistakes in my life, but letting them go was my biggest."

Ashley felt a twinge of envy for this other woman who still held Tenny's heart. She changed the subject. "Your art is magnificent. It's so powerful."

"They remind me of my purpose and my own good fortune." Tenny handed Ashley her juice, turned and walked away. Ashley would move no closer tonight.

▼

The conversation with Margo had not gone well. She didn't want Ashley staying with Tenny and wasn't convinced that the whole thing had been unavoidable. Feeling defensive, Ashley cut her off and hung up. She joined Tenny, who was seated in the bay window, gazing into the night.

"I guess your girlfriend doesn't like this arrangement much."

"She doesn't understand."

"Sounds like she's not feeling secure about your commitment."

"Look, I love her," Ashley snapped. "I tell her that all the time. What more does she want from me?"

Tenny stood. "Maybe she wants more than the words. Maybe she wants to *feel* your love." Tenny was gone before Ashley could respond.

The three investigators spent the next morning making sure there were no other possible suspects with access to the same information. Once they had eliminated any other possibilities, they began to focus on the two they had. Fortunately, both men worked for a public agency, so that many of the actual business records were public information. Mindful of what the court would say, they had also spoken with the District Attorney before digging deeper into the suspects' lives.

After several hours, Steve placed the phone down and leaned back in his chair, stretching his huge arms up and resting his head against his intertwined fingers. He looked smug. "I got him."

"Come on, Steve, what are you talking about?" Ashley was getting tired. "I'm not in the mood to play games. I've been on this phone the whole damn day, and my story just keeps getting worse and worse."

"Well, mine gets better and better. All this busywork has paid off, gal. I went through every back door so I wouldn't tip this bastard off, and I got him." Steve was still leaning back, but his tone became intense. "I finally got to his itinerary for the last eight months. That bastard has been in the area on business during each hit. He works with the various colleges and travels all the time. He may be old, Ashley, but he's smart. We got him now, though."

Ashley had eliminated her own suspect after confirming that he had had alibis for several of the hits. As she listened to Steve, her stomach started to turn with the adrenaline she had not felt since leaving patrol. She knew that he felt the same way. It was the cop's intuition, that sixth sense.

"His itinerary is being faxed to us, and it gets better. He'll be in our city day after tomorrow. I think the tables are about to turn in our favor."

At that moment, Tenny burst through the door to her office. "Idiots! I can't believe their management mentality. They couldn't see an opportunity to do something right if it hit them in the damn face." She was sure her muscles would rip from her bones with tension. She paced the office, muttering obscenities, until Steve placed his imposing frame in her path.

"Tenny, talk to us. What did they say?"

"They said that our team was not cost-effective. They think that we've had enough of an opportunity to work together and that it doesn't seem to be assisting the investigation. They claim that it's just making this one of the most expensive investigations of the past ten years. When I pointed out that we had some suspects, they said, 'Great, then anybody can take over the cases now and do the necessary follow-up.' They want to break us up, put me back on homicides, and ship you two back to your own department for God knows what."

Steve collapsed back into his seat. "They can't do this," pleaded Ashley. "Tenny, you need to go back to them. We know who it is. Steve's guy has been in the area during every hit. We're so close! You can't let them do this."

Tenny stopped pacing when she heard the news. "Steve, do we really have this guy pinned down?"

"It looks good, Tenny. We're close."

"Shit, I can't believe they're being so stupid, but I don't think there's anything I can say. All they care about is how much damn money it's costing them. I've already tried every argument I know, and they've got their minds made up." Tenny went and stood in a corner of the office, defeated at a moment when she could have won.

Nobody spoke. After several moments, Steve suddenly began to smile and leaned back in his chair, resuming his cocky, smug pose. "I'm surprised at you two, especially you, Tenny." Tenny glared at him from her corner, wondering what he was getting at now.

Steve continued, "You taught me about the power of your community, and now you're battling on your own instead of using your resources."

Steve pulled out a stack of business cards which he had collected from their community meeting. Tenny watched him go to work. His words, the same words she had used so often, seemed foreign to her. She kicked herself for not thinking of the obvious, that critical link which she had used so often before and ignored this time. It was her turn to feel embarrassed and humbled.

▼

Steve hung up the phone after about thirty minutes and gave Ashley and Tenny a wicked grin. "I think that those three calls should do the trick. Where's your Captain's office? I've got to see this."

Tenny led them through the division to the corner office. The secretary was already busy on the phone taking messages and placing callers on hold. Every available outside line was lit by inquiries. Through the Captain's open door they could hear him assuring a concerned citizen that their department had no plan of backing off one bit on this terrible serial rapist investigation and that they had every intention of doing whatever it took to apprehend him.

Steve turned to Tenny and Ashley. "Your community is not only powerful, but also well connected. I'd love to see the names in that pile of messages and know who he's talking to right now." They continued past the Captain's office and back to Tenny's.

"Well, that should take care of our little management problem. Now can we get back to the business of getting this asshole." Steve sat down, ready to formulate their next step.

▼

Their work carried them into the evening. None of them seemed to mind. They needed to backtrack and find the evidence on this guy. He must have had some type of personal contact with each victim, enough to pick the women out as lesbians.

Tenny would start interviewing the Bay Area victims the next day. Ashley would fly home early in the morning and talk to the women from her jurisdiction. Steve would follow the suspect in the afternoon as he left the loan office. There was no way to be sure that he would check into his hotel before doing something suspicious or illegal. Steve had to be there when it happened. Tenny had insisted on notifying the California Highway Patrol, and they had generously offered to assist Steve in the mobile surveillance as the suspect traveled down the state.

Steve called his department and had the surveillance on 113 Palo Verde staffed with two additional officers. They would be ready for anything this jerk tried.

Tenny thought such a long day would be too much for Steve. But he almost pleaded, "Tenny, I know that this is our guy, and I know that he's going to do something soon after he gets into town. I want to be there when he does it. Give me all the backup you want, but I'm going to be on him."

Ashley pouted. "I know what I'm going to be doing is important, but I want to be in on the end when the handcuffs go on."

"We know that, but if we're going to be able to hold him on some damn misdemeanor prowling case, we're going to need more evidence on him. We need that connection." Steve knew that Ashley was used to snapping those handcuffs on. She would have to get used to doing all the work so that somebody else could make the arrest.

▼

They had finished the long day by making a list of questions for each woman. In addition, Tenny had made arrangements with the local FBI and the loan office manager to slip a small electronic transmitter in with the suspect's files. This would allow Steve to follow him without having to maintain visual contact. Between the CHP officers and Steve's tracking system, she felt confident that they would not get burned or lose him.

"I'm starving. Where are we going to eat?" Ashley was packing the reports into her briefcase.

Steve was almost out the door. "I don't know about you, ladies, but I have a date, and she's picking where we eat."

Steve didn't even see her coming. Ashley covered about fifteen feet in two powerful strides and was on him. Before he could defend himself, he was in a firm control hold.

Tenny laughed as Ashley dragged Steve back into the office and shut the door. "Where do you think you're going so fast? We want the scoop."

"What scoop? It's a date, that's all."

"When have you had time to meet anybody up here?" Tenny was instantly inquisitive.

"Steve's got a date. Steve's got a date." Ashley was doing an impressive imitation of an adolescent.

"I met her early yesterday morning when I went to Cassey Dillion's office to speak to her about the case."

Tenny looked surprised. "*The* Cassey Dillion? What were you doing at her office?"

"I told you. She wanted to know about the case. She feels that she needs to come out and add her influence and some political arm-twisting to our investigation."

"Come out? I had no idea. Whoa, I mean, I have wondered at times, but she's so private." Tenny was startled.

"Well, she was the first person I called today, and she was probably the one your Captain was speaking with while we discreetly eavesdropped. I don't think she'll be able to keep her private life concealed for much longer. But she was ready to take a stand for herself and her peers. I tell you, she's a dynamic woman."

Ashley interrupted, "That's not who you have a date with, though."

"No, it's her secretary. While I was waiting, she was talking to me about the case. She was really concerned about many of her friends and worried about Cassey. She's an extremely intelligent woman and we had a coffee together after my meeting. She was impressed with how sensitive I am."

Tenny's and Ashley's laughter rang with sarcasm. "Oh, yeah, your sensitivity drew me to you instantly, too." Tenny was shaking her head in disbelief.

"I guess I'm just a changed man."

The smile left Tenny's face. "Really? So the next time your buddies back at the department are ragging on lesbians and making all those typical crude jokes, you're going to speak up and educate them or tell them to shove it?"

Silence swept through the room, a flash flood of reality. All three investigators knew the answer to Tenny's question. Steve thought about that evening in the weight room. It was as if Tenny knew. He couldn't look at either of his partners.

Ashley broke the strained silence. "We understand, Steve. It's not easy to be different. It's even more difficult to help others change their own beliefs. We know you care, and that's enough." She reached up and gave him a kiss on the cheek.

Tenny didn't move. She was so tired of people molding their personal beliefs to match those of the people they were with at that moment. How could prejudice ever really be fought if people couldn't even form their own values, judgments, and beliefs, then stick to them no matter what group they were in?

▼

"You were kind of rough on Steve. You know he's trying." Ashley had waited until they had settled in at their table before bringing up the subject.

Tenny looked at Ashley. Her expressionless face made Ashley uncomfortable. Finally she responded, "You're right, I just get so frustrated sometimes. Steve has been wonderful, like many people are when they really get to spend time with somebody they were sure they hated simply because of the color of their skin or something. But I'm so tired of the little steps. I want hundreds of people to understand, not just Steve."

"Starting with small steps is better than not starting at all."

"Ah, such wisdom from a youngster." Tenny dropped her chin in mock coyness, smiling up at Ashley from under her bangs.

"OK, Miss Tenacity, tell me something. With all your wisdom, why are you still a homicide detective and not the captain that people say you could have been?"

"Well, that's rather a personal question. Maybe I just don't have what it takes to be an administrator."

"Bullshit!"

Tenny sat back in her chair, tilted her head, curled her lips in, squinted her eyes, and looked at Ashley. *What the hell,* she thought, *tell this woman what she wants to know. She's the closest thing to a friend that you've had in quite some time.*

"I left the FBI because they didn't appreciate my selection of bedmates, and I was tired of hiding everything about myself. So I decided that I would go to a municipal department where I would be accepted for who I am and move up through the ranks. I had the education, and everybody told me I had the talent, so I ended up here planning to get on the career fast track. I had to start at the bottom on the streets, but I knew that wouldn't last long. But I had never worked in patrol before, and I was in for a surprise."

Ashley listened keenly, not wanting to miss anything that Tenny was willing to offer. "I fell in love with the job of the street cop. The meaningful interaction that you have with people, both good and bad. You can't find that in any other job or position. The people on the beat meant something to me, and I looked forward to seeing them. Law enforcement took on a whole new importance for me. Being near people and the real world is what became worthwhile to me. I never got around to putting in for promotions. The streets are where I belong."

Ashley noticed that Tenny would no longer make eye contact with her. She was staring at her wine glass, lost in her own thoughts. Ashley thought back to the art in Tenny's home. "I also heard that there is a story behind your nickname. Tell me it."

"It's not a happy story and not one I care to discuss." The walls around Elizabeth Mendoza came crashing down. Ashley had once again come too close, but the distance separating them was narrowing. Ashley vowed once again to be patient.

Over dinner Ashley gathered her courage. "I have to admit something," she said, not waiting for Tenny's response. "From the first time I saw you, I've been debating with myself about exactly what your ethnic background is and I'm willing to give in now and let you tell me."

"I've been called it all, so I'm whatever you'd like me to be."

Ashley sensed that Tenny was teasing her this time. "I'd like you to be my friend," she persisted, making Tenny blush. "Talk to me, because I'm not going away and you're not walking away anymore. I want to be your friend."

Tenny thought of all the people who had tried to be her friend the last two years. She looked into Ashley's eyes, emerald green and translucent, like the crest of an ocean wave with the sun shining through. Tenny had always been calmed by the ocean. It was time to trust again.

"I'm half Black and half Mexican. My parents met in 1952 while my mom was in college. My dad worked in a local pharmacy. He only got that job because he looked more European than Mexican. My mom's family threw a tantrum when they found out my mom was engaged to him. They had worked so hard to give her all the comforts of a middle-class upbringing and to ease her acceptance into white culture. It infuriated them that she would throw all that away on some 'spic.' But none of the family threats or exile that my parents experienced tore them apart. They taught us that it's not what you are, but who you are. If you feel good about yourself and what you give, then the rest of the world can go to hell."

"They sound like good people."

"The best. My family has always supported me, no matter what. I'm lucky, in our family blood really does mean more than anything else."

Tears began to well up in Ashley's eyes. Tenny wondered how she lived without the love of her family.

"Ashley, have you seen your mom since you left home?"

Ashley's whole body tensed in an effort to stop her tears. She reached for the charm around her neck. She wanted to talk, but not where everybody could see her pain.

"Can we leave?"

"Of course."

They left and began to walk towards the bay. Ashley was still toying with the charm as they walked.

"What is that charm?" Tenny had noticed it before.

"It's called a *labrys*. It's an ancient Greek symbol for Amazon women. I guess it's supposed to symbolize women's power and strength when they stand together in battle. My mom gave it to me when I was young to symbolize our own strength even though we were all alone." She paused for a moment. "I never went back. In fact, I avoid that whole area of town. I couldn't take the hurt and rejection twice. I think about her all the time, though. I'm constantly checking the computer at work to make sure nothing has happened to her."

"How do you know that you would get hurt?"

"Tenny, if she wanted me back in her life, she would come find me."

Tenny stopped walking. Ashley turned back to her.

"How would she find you?" Tenny asked. "Does she know you're a cop? Is your phone number listed? Or because she's a mother, she's just supposed to find you by tracking your vibes?"

Tears rushed down Ashley's cheeks. "Goddamn it, Tenny!" she snapped. "My name and picture have been in the paper dozens of times for arrests that I've made. She reads the paper. She *could* find me if she wanted."

Tenny felt terrible. She reached out to Ashley and pulled her close, while Ashley struggled to stop the tears.

"I'm sorry. Don't worry, my parents will adopt you. They adopt all my friends. Of course, that means weekly calls from Mom."

Ashley laughed in Tenny's arms as the words settled in. She felt comfortable and happy. Tenny was her friend.

They began to walk again, and Tenny changed the subject.

"What do you see in the future for you and Margo?"

Ashley threw her head back and her arms out to her sides. "Shit, Mendoza, you really know how to pick topics for conversation!"

"Hey, I'm just trying to be your friend." Tenny grinned at her.

"I don't know what I see in the future. Day to day was fine with her until you came along." Tenny gave Ashley a questioning look. "She thinks I have a thing for you, Ms. Tenacity."

"You mean you don't?" Tenny tried to look crushed.

"Very funny. Actually, it took me realizing that I didn't to really make me understand that I do love Margo. But I'm still not clear on this commitment stuff."

"Maybe you're scared of risking the loss of another person you love. By convincing yourself that the two of you don't really have anything special, there's no risk."

They talked about how love feels and how you know it's time for a lifetime commitment. They talked about Margo and how much Ashley loved her. They talked about what Ashley wanted and dreamed, all of which seemed to include Margo. Finally Ashley stopped and stared out at the bay.

She announced, "You know, I really love Margo. You were right last night, I need to express my love more. I don't know why I've been so frightened, maybe it was being scared of losing another person that I love. But if I don't let myself love her totally, I'll lose her anyway. Why is love so complex?"

Tenny stood next to her. "Because that's how we make it. Follow your instincts and your heart. God gave us brains to think with, not to love with."

Tenny swung around and looked in both directions. "Shit, girl, your love-filled heart carried us a long way from home. I don't suppose clicking your heels three times would get us home?"

Ashley felt free of doubt. Bursting with happiness, she grabbed Tenny and gave her a big bear hug, then turned and walked away. Tonight was perfect. She had finally completely released her love for Margo, she had left Miss Tenacity watching *her* heels, and she was on the track of this asshole hurting women.

Ashley returned home at noon the next day and went right into the department. There were several victims to contact, and she didn't want to waste any time. However, there was one thing she had to do first.

Once inside the office, she immediately called the courthouse. "Department Fifteen, please. Hi, Teddy, it's Ashley, can I speak with Margo?"

"Sorry kid, she's not handling the cases today. Do you want me to transfer you downstairs?"

"Sure, thanks Teddy."

▼

The police report was open on Margo's desk. She was leaning back in her chair, with her chin resting lightly on the eraser of her freshly sharpened pencil. Anybody walking past her office would assume she was deep in thought while working on an important case. They would be wrong.

Margo was obsessed. She had spent a long night trying to reach Ashley, waiting to hear from her, sitting alone in the dark. This morning, for the first time in her career, she had asked another deputy DA to handle her calendar. The telephone rang and Margo picked it up reluctantly.

There was a long pause before Margo announced herself. She sounded tired and flat. "Hey, babe, you all right?" Ashley missed her more than ever.

"I'm fine. Where are you?" Margo interrogated her like a hostile witness.

"I'm home, well, at the office. I just arrived. I wanted to surprise you."

"What enabled you to tear yourself away from your new *friend?*" Margo's sarcasm slashed at Ashley's patience.

"Hey, I don't deserve that."

"Oh, of course, she's probably standing beside you right now. After all, you two are *partners.*"

"Where is this childish jealousy coming from?" Ashley snapped.

"You're calling *me* childish. That's a joke. *You're* the one running around with a juvenile crush on Tenny. She's all you talk about, all you think about. Oh, by the way, how was last night? I noticed neither one of you could manage to pick up the phone."

So Margo had been the three hang-ups on Tenny's machine.

"Margo, please don't be like this," Ashley pleaded. "I love you and I spent all last night talking about just how much you mean to me. I missed you."

Margo ignored her. "I can't go on like this. You want your freedom to spend time with whoever you like, doing whatever, but at the same time you want to claim you love me. Well, that's not good enough."

Ashley couldn't stand any more. "I can't talk to you. All you ever want to talk about is forever, and there ain't nothing forever, babe, including me." Ashley slammed the phone down, gathered her case files, and left. She had important work to do and no time to waste dealing with Margo.

Later that evening, after Ashley had finished interviewing all the women, she realized she'd gotten nowhere. Several of her victims had never had any contact with the federal college loan office, and none had met or spoken with anybody from that particular office. Ashley was going to have to call Tenny and see what she had discovered. Maybe the questions they asked were wrong. On the other hand, maybe Tenny had figured it all out by now. Anyway, Steve was probably going to catch their suspect in the act tonight and make the arrest. Ashley still couldn't accept that she would miss the end.

She decided to call Tenny in the morning. Tonight she had a more important issue to handle. Her silly fight with Margo had been on her mind all day. Now as she drove home, her apology and their love for each other were all she could think about. Ashley was nervous, but she believed that was a good sign. Margo was Ashley's true love and Ashley was ready to make her feel that way.

When Ashley pulled into the driveway, Margo's car wasn't there. It was past eight and Ashley knew that Margo wasn't still at work. Ashley was disappointed but not surprised. Margo often went out with her work buddies when she wanted to avoid a bad situation or she was angry. Being hung up on would probably keep her away late into the night.

Ashley stayed up as late as she could, waiting for Margo to come home. She ate, unpacked, and spent time thinking about how she was going to love Margo the right way for the rest of her life. Their fight had not dampened her love for more than an hour. They were going to make it forever. Ashley fell asleep feeling more secure in her future than she had in years.

▼

"Oh, God, not again." Tenny had awakened with a death clench on her pillow, drenched with sweat. Every muscle in her body ached. The same dream, the one that had haunted her for years, always came when something awful happened. This time it was so real, so close. Tenny was still frightened although she was completely awake. Something was terribly wrong and it was close to her.

▼

She was in her teddy bear undershorts and the pink cutoff sweatshirt she always wore when sleeping alone. The floor was cool on her bare feet and the gun in her hand sent shivers up her arm. She had heard a noise and had gotten up to investigate, grabbing her gun more out of habit than concern. It was probably Margo finally arriving home.

She came down the stairs and went to the front window to check the driveway. Margo's car wasn't there. Ashley turned her back to the window to face the house. Something was wrong. Her stomach was tensing, the grip on her gun tightening, and her mind was forcing her into the familiar police awareness. There had been a noise, she knew that much.

Ashley recalled Tenny describing how one of the victims had convinced herself that the noise had been nothing. Ashley knew better. She decided to check the rest of the house. The gun stayed at her side as she began to turn on lights and work her way through the downstairs. Ashley flicked on the hall light as she walked towards the kitchen. Then she froze, her weapon snapped up into a ready position, extended in front of her, slightly below her line of vision.

A pane of glass in the kitchen door had been smashed and the door stood partially open. Ashley threw her back against the wall to allow herself to see in both directions. It was him. The bastard was in her house.

Quickly Ashley evaluated her options. Get to a phone and call for backup or get the hell out of the house. She cursed. No matter what she chose to do, she had to move from this spot. She slid carefully down the wall towards the kitchen. Straining to see the whole left side of the kitchen in the darkness, she flipped her body across the hall to check the right side. The room was empty.

Now the pantry was at her back. The only place left to hide. Ashley had to check. Maybe he had already fled. Her heart raced, pumping blood too quickly to her head, making her dizzy. She took a deep breath and tried to steady her shaking hands.

Ashley lunged around the corner, whirling to face the pantry. A black-covered arm grabbed her gun.

He used her own tremendous momentum against her. Swinging her past him towards his hiding place, he held up her outstretched arms and drove her entire body into the wall next to the pantry. She felt the gun discharge at the end of her outstretched arms. Then her wrist exploded in a collision with the wall. The pain was unbearable. Her fear was overwhelming. Disarmed, locked in a bear hug, she realized this would not work. She had lost the upper hand and there was no backup on the way. But Ashley was not just another victim for this asshole. She *was a cop* and she was trained to survive—no matter what the cost.

Ashley jerked her legs up and pushed out from the wall. The seconds that they were airborne seemed to last minutes. His hold broke the moment they hit the floor. Ashley inflicted a sharp jab to his ribs and twisted free.

There was no time to find the gun. Ashley dove back at him, grabbing his left arm in an attempt to apply a control hold, but her wrist failed her. She was losing.

Standing up as if she wasn't even there, he flung himself backwards, smashing Ashley into the kitchen counter. Again Ashley felt her body crumbling as the edge of the counter broke several ribs.

He spun around to face her and began to rip at her clothes. Ashley struggled for breath, for conscious thought, for the strength to fight. He tore her shorts from her body. Crushing her beneath his weight, holding her with one arm, he moved his other hand between her legs and touched her. Then he unzipped his pants and she felt him against her.

Ashley was frantic to stop him. Her arms broke free and she began to tear at his mask, poking at his eyes with her weakened hand. With her good hand she reached down his back and raked upwards until she came to the tape, then she tore with all her strength. She was at least going to see this bastard's face. She would get him for this unless he killed her first.

He screamed and stepped back as the tape ripped away from his skin. The mask came off over his head. Ashley gasped, "I know you. I know you!"

He slammed his fist into her gut and then into her face. The blows sent her to the ground, but Ashley refused to give up consciousness; she was going to fight. She felt a quick, sharp pain across the back of her neck and knew it wasn't over yet. She pushed herself up from the floor, but he was gone. The house was silent. Nothing was left but the mask.

He had fled, but she had seen him and she knew him. Ashley reached for the phone, although every part of her body protested movement. She ignored her body's complaints. The fight had just begun.

▼

Steve was losing his patience. The guy he was following had not done anything remotely suspicious. Maybe Tenny was right, maybe this was the wrong guy. She still hadn't found any information that would have allowed him to pick out the victims as lesbians. None of the women remembered any personal contact with him.

But everything seemed so perfect. The right blood type, the right physical description, in the right places and at the right times. Steve believed in coincidences, but that was too much. This guy was simply better than they had anticipated.

What had gone wrong? Maybe the suspect knew he was hot.

Maybe the locals had screwed up and tipped him off. He *had* to be the right guy.

It had been a long drive down here and then a long night of watching nothing. The suspect had gone to his hotel in the early evening and had not come back out. They had all the exits covered and several officers in plain clothes inside the hotel. They had really blown the budget on this little operation, and Steve knew that if nothing came of it their investigation team would be broken apart.

"Shit, what the hell?" The phone rang suddenly, and Steve's heart dropped to his knees. "Damn these fancy dooda gadgets. Where the hell do they hide that thing in this car?" He checked under seats and in the glove compartment, finally finding the phone behind the front passenger seat. "Pretty nifty, I'll have to mention this one to my Captain."

Steve lost his breath again when the unexpected voice on the line belonged to his Captain. He sounded as if his stomach problems were acting up again. "Steve, you get your ass back over here now! That asshole you're supposedly sitting on hit tonight. This time he made it personal between him and our department." Steve could hear the choked anger, the Captain's voice teetering between tears and screams. "The bastard attacked Ashley. He beat the shit out of her. I'm not going to discuss it with you on the phone. Get over here!" The line went dead. The last command had sounded more like a plea.

Steve put the phone back and grasped the ignition key. His mind was reeling, his heart pounding with rage. Why Ashley? Then he remembered.

"Because she's different. She's a lesbian." As he said the word aloud for the first time, the cruel absurdity of the crime struck him and he laughed, then cried with shame, with pain, with fear. All the hate and violence he had seen in his career came flooding back. He was frightened. Now the hate had forced itself into his own life, and the victim was his friend.

15

He slammed the door shut and barricaded it with his body. His skin was clammy with cold sweat, despite the heat outside. His stomach was convulsing. His body shook.

"Fuck, I can't believe I let that bitch see my face. I let her win. Damn, why did I run? I could have still beat her. I could've taught her a lesson she'd never forget."

He walked across his apartment and into the bathroom, grabbing the sink. The pain in his shoulder was intense. She had partially dislocated it during their struggle. Again he cursed his weakness. He started the faucet and splashed cool water on his face. Bringing his head up he looked directly into the mirror.

"Oh, God, oh, God, she saw my face. You fucking fool, she saw your *face.*" The mirror shattered as he struck it, trying to erase his image. The image he was sure was captured now in her mind. He stepped from the bathroom and began to unleash his frustrations and fear on the inanimate objects throughout his apartment.

"Why did I run? I could have killed her. God, I should have killed her, that cocky cunt. I should have done it nice and slow with her and then ended her miserable, backwards life. Now what am I going to do? She saw my face! She'll remember, and it won't take long to track me down."

He stopped his tantrum and clenched his fist to his chest. Control, that was the key, he had to regain control. Either go back and kill the bitch or else run. Leave the country, leave this mess he had created. There were other women in other countries that needed his attention. He knew that this ungodly love some American women had was not just a curse of this country. Maybe he should go abroad and educate the others. The thought made him smile.

He removed Ashley's labrys from his pocket and turned it slowly in his hand. He was going to prove who really had the power. "I won't let that bitch beat me!" He remembered his mother with rage.

The only sure victory was to defeat them and make them love him or make them unable to love anybody else ever again. Now he knew what he would do.

16

By the time Steve got to the airport, Tenny had already managed to get a flight down. When she found him waiting, she showed no emotion whatsoever. Steve respected her silence. When they arrived at the hospital Tenny hung back, hesitant to enter Ashley's room. Steve went in first. Ashley's right wrist was in a cast, and the fingers which emerged from the end of the crisp white plaster were a shocking contrast, deep red and purple, and badly swollen. Ashley's other wrist, though unwrapped, looked just as bad. Her face was bruised and her lip was cut in several places. The bastard had even left impressions of his fingers on her neck where he had tried to choke her into submission. Steve was thankful he couldn't see anything more.

Steve nodded to Margo, who was seated on the other side of the bed, then gently reached out to touch Ashley's face. Ashley had been staring ahead, unaware of anything around her. When Steve touched her, she turned and her expressionless eyes met his. She smiled, briefly, but her eyes were searching for Tenacity.

Tenny had entered the room but was still hanging back. Her memories were nearly unbearable. She had let somebody down again. She had missed something in this investigation, something that could have prevented this attack from happening. There was nothing she could say. She was tired of having to offer only words. She wanted this bastard.

Tenny listened to Ashley reassure Steve and she realized that, for her, this attack had been different from the rest. Ashley was a cop and she had fought like one. No cop ever wants to become a victim. Tenny knew that Ashley had done everything in her power to end the nightmare in her own home. The bruises she bore came from performing her duty. All good cops wore them once in a while. Tenny came towards the bed.

"Girl, you look like shit, but I know he looks just as bad. Now tell me how to catch this pervert."

Ashley was relieved to know that Tenny still respected her. She reached for Tenny with her cast-heavy arm, and Tenny responded with a kiss on the cheek. Ashley dropped her arm on Tenny's back and held her close. Tenny whispered in her ear, "We're going to get him now, babe. I know it in my soul." When Ashley released her, Tenny saw the look of burning determination she had only met in one other place—the mirror.

Ashley said something in a low growl that neither Steve nor Tenny could make out. She repeated, "I got his mask off and I saw his face. I *know* the bastard. I've seen him before, but I can't remember where." Ashley began to cry.

"Ashley, you're trying too hard. What you need to do is rest, and it will come to you," Steve encouraged her.

"I can't rest. Every time I close my eyes I see his face, but I can't remember. It's driving me crazy. If he hits again it will be all my fault."

"All right, let's talk about him, the attack, and your life. Maybe it'll trigger your memory." Steve was anxious to jog her memory anyway.

▼

Tenny excused herself as Steve and Ashley went over the attack. In the hall she landed an explosive punch against the opposite wall, pivoted away, and began to pace the hall. How could this asshole get so lucky again? They had all worked so hard and were so close. How could this be happening? She knew how hard Ashley had fought. Shit, all you had to do was look at her. Yet with all the effort, the fight, and the purpose, why was luck once again protecting him by stealing Ashley's memory?

Tenny was still allowing her anger to dissipate in the public anonymity of the hallway when Margo stepped in front of her. This was their first meeting, although they had heard plenty about each other.

Margo had silently observed the touching moment when Tenny and Ashley had found strength together in what she considered a public display of their love. Margo's jealousy clouded her ability to recognize an expression of unrelenting friendship. She only saw a threat and she stepped into the hall-way, ready to end this affair right now.

"Detective Mendoza, I am only going to tell you this once. You stay away from Ashley. If you hadn't been trying to come between us this never would have happened. I would have been there last night. I'm not young and impressionable like Ashley. You don't fool me or astound me, and you most defi-nitely don't intimidate me. So why don't you just fly back to where you belong. Our police department and the District Attorney's office will complete this investigation, since the great Tenacity has been useless thus far."

Tenny closed the distance between them. "You stupid bitch! All Ashley ever talks about is you. She loves you so much that she has trouble understanding it. But your own insecurities and possessiveness interfere with the love between you two. She was ready to commit to you forever, but you were so blinded by your own imagination that you missed it. I had nothing but respect for you from listening to Ashley, but right at this moment I find you repulsive." Tenny stormed past her toward the exit.

She wasn't about to give the attorney the satisfaction of cross-examination or argument. Margo watched her stride away.

▼

The lights from the street below seeped into the darkness of the hospital room through the open window. If she had cared to look, Ashley could just barely have made out the vase of flowers placed on a corner table. Right now she was not looking at anything. Her vision was within, reviewing her life day by day since she had become a cop. Where had she seen that face?

The telephone disturbed the hunt.

"Hello."

"I want you to stop thinking about him and get some sleep right now. That's my first and last order as the leader of this investigative team." Ashley now noticed the flowers that Tenny had sent. She smiled, it was good to hear Tenny's voice.

"I know that you and Steve worked on figuring this out all afternoon with no luck, but that doesn't mean it's lost forever."

Ashley whined, "That's what Steve said too."

"What else did Steve say?"

"He said that the answer is probably trapped in my subconscious and as soon as I go to sleep it'll come out in my dreams."

"It'll be a nightmare, but the man's right. So why did I know you would still be awake?" Tenny tried to sound light.

Ashley became intense, almost desperate. "Tenny, I *can't* sleep. I've got to figure this out, or it will be the biggest mistake of my life. He's got to be stopped, and I'm the only one that can do it now. I'll never sleep again if he hurts another woman."

"He's probably halfway across the country by now, running like hell."

"Tenny, you don't really believe that. We don't know *how* I know him. He may not know I'm a cop. He may feel safe because he hasn't got a record and he assumes there is no place for me to pick out his face. Plus, even if he is running, what's to keep him from starting over again in some other city? You were

144

even afraid of that happening before. Come on, Tenny, he's not stupid and neither am I."

Tenny realized that Ashley had learned quickly as an investigator. She had fit together all the little pieces of information they had been able to scavenge, and she was reading them correctly. "You're right, Ashley, he's still out there. But you're wrong about something else. If he hits again before we find him, it won't be your fault. Many uncontrollable factors have fallen on his side so far. The fact that you can't remember where you've seen his face before is just another one. It's temporary, Ashley. Soon the luck is going to turn."

"I know you're right, but I still feel like I blew it. It *will* be all my fault. Don't you understand?"

There was a long silence. Ashley could picture Tenny's clenched teeth and her eyes shifting around the room.

"Tenny? Tell me about the old woman. The one in your living room. I know she had something to do with your nickname."

Tenny began to speak, but she sounded different, susceptible. "She's *my* burden of guilt. I was a new officer with the department, and I was just starting to realize how much working with people meant to me. One day I saw the three of them walking along near the park. For some reason they tugged at my heart, so I stopped to talk to them.

"Her name was Pearl and she was definitely a rare find. The girls were her granddaughters. Pearl had moved from back East to help her daughter with the children after their father disappeared. She gave up everything she had to help her family. Yet when she arrived, it didn't take Pearl long to figure out that her own baby had changed.

"The home had been physically abusive and the girls were being sexually molested by a live-in boyfriend. There were drugs, fights, and never enough money.

"Finally, Pearl took the children and left.

"They had been on the streets for about three months when I met them. Pearl was starting to feel as if she had made a terrible mistake. We managed to find them shelter on a week-to-week basis, but that wasn't enough."

Tenny pushed herself to continue. "Good old Mom decided that she wanted the girls back. It wasn't love, she needed them to collect her welfare check. Well, by that time, Pearl had many supporters in the community, and everybody was working with her to find a way for her to keep the children. Pearl was taking care of them as best she could. They were going to school. They always had food and clothes. But most of all they loved their grandmother and were loved by her."

Tenny took a deep breath. "I tried to protect Pearl from her daughter. Then one day I found her in an alley, sitting against the wall in the cold with her girls. She told me that her daughter's boyfriend had found her at the shelter and she was frightened. She had barely gotten away and wanted to stay on the streets that night. I asked her to come stay with me, but she refused. Her pride had its limits."

Another deep breath and Tenny's voice began to quiver. "She grabbed my hand and told me to stop worrying so much. I could tell she was scared and needed help, but she smiled and pushed me away. I didn't want to leave her, but I didn't know what else to do. I didn't know how far to take my responsibilities."

Another long silence. Ashley knew what was coming. She could hear Tenny trying to control the tears and her own began to flow.

"Pearl was killed that night and the children disappeared. The daughter and the boyfriend seemed clear, it's still an unsolved case. Nobody blamed me. Everybody said that I had done everything and more than what is expected of a cop. But I know I could have done more, not as a cop, but as a human being. It changed my life. I lost my confidence. I lost my lover. Shit, it almost destroyed me."

Strength sprang into Tenny's voice. "I haven't had an unsolved case since then, and I'm not about to start with this one. Get some sleep." She hung up.

Tenny and Steve arrived at the hospital early the next morning. Ashley had not gotten much sleep, and she recognized the same signs of stress and exhaustion on their faces.

Ashley reached for her charm, but it was gone. "What happened? Shit! He hit again, didn't he? No! God, why can't I remember?" Ashley had feared this all night as she sat helpless in the hospital, torturing herself for her inability to remember.

Tenny explained to Ashley that the man had traveled north again and raped another woman last night. Then she let the silence descend around them. Tenny didn't know how to go on. She knew all too well how the news would affect her partner. She touched Steve's back, asking him to finish.

He spoke quietly. "Ashley, we have a real problem. He broke his pattern this time. It might be a copycat, but I think that he's sending a message." Steve hesitated, watching Ashley's face. "He killed this victim."

Ashley began to shake. Steve stood helplessly as Tenny stepped past him.

Tenny was sobbing. She leaned down to Ashley and they grabbed onto each other, weeping for all the victims they didn't know and the ones that were still waiting, for the unbelievable insanity of it all. Finally, Steve understood that their tears were also for each other. He gently kissed them both on the cheek.

"I'm sorry." It was all he could offer. The three of them sat quietly holding hands for almost an hour, knowing that their lives would never be the same after this case. The release of frustration, pain, and sorrow served to clear their minds. They all felt like giving up, but knew they were the only answer to this problem.

"We have to get up there, we'll keep you informed. The doctor said you will be ready to go home in a couple of days," Tenny said at last.

"Tenny, I'm not staying here. I'm going with you. I need to, I'm the best clue we have so far. I can't just sit here. Tenny, please, I must find him." Ashley was already getting out of bed.

"Ashley, you can barely move, and I'm sure that your department has you placed on restricted duty."

Ashley turned to Steve. "What do you think, Steve, am I on restricted duty?"

"No way, you've got to be comatose to get put on light duty in this department. You look fine." The partners exchanged a brief smile.

Tenny made another attempt. "Look, checking you out will take forever, and you don't even have your weapon."

Steve produced a semi-automatic and Ashley's badge from his bag. "Who needs to check out? They won't even notice her missing until it's time to feed her lunch. Let's get going."

Ashley dressed in the clothes Margo had brought the day before. On the way out the door, Steve remarked, "Hope you've been practicing your weak hand shooting."

Ashley fired back, "I would have, if I had a weak hand like you do, Steve."

Tenny thought how cops always found a way to laugh. It was either laugh or spend a lifetime crying. Tenny found the teasing exchange between her partners refreshing. It wouldn't last long.

▼

They moved through the airport with calm urgency. Ashley was struggling to keep up with Steve and Tenny. The pain in her ribs made breathing difficult. A disturbing sensation in her chest was also trying to get her attention. Slowing down to see if it would go away, Ashley noticed her surroundings as a chill went through her body. Tenny was right. She should have stayed at the hospital.

Ashley felt lightheaded. What was wrong? Catching up to Tenny and Steve at the check-in desk, she felt her body slightly out of control, on the verge of some attack.

It came to her so unexpectedly that it almost brought her to her knees. Steve, next to her, caught Ashley before she fell.

"It was here!" she gasped. "He flirted with me here! The bastard works here!"

18

Steve was first to the desk. He practically pounced on the woman standing at the computer terminal. There was no introduction, no explanation, and no hesitation on his part. He had forgotten all the requirements of communication in his frantic rush for information about the suspect.

"I want to talk to whoever's in charge of TRANS-CAL personnel, and I want to talk to him now."

The reservation clerk had no idea what was going on, but the counter between them gave her courage.

"I'm sorry, sir, but you'll have to explain the problem to me."

As the reservation clerk and Steve squared off, Tenny walked up calmly. "Hello, please let me explain."

Tenny identified herself with her badge as she continued. "I'm Detective Mendoza, and we are trying to locate one of your employees. He's not in trouble, but it is important that we speak to him as soon as possible. You probably even know him. The problem is that we were only given his description. He's supposed to be quite attractive, over six feet tall, with brown hair. I'm told that he's quite charming."

The clerk eyed Tenny, who noticed her hesitation. "I know this is an unusual circumstance, but there's a family emergency and the only information that our officer was able to obtain on the way to the hospital was the young man's place of employment. The description came from a photograph in the home. The poor gentleman, we think it's his father, he didn't have any identification that we could find."

Pretty weak story, thought Tenny, but the clerk fell for it.

"Oh, his name's Thomas Whittington. He's a terribly sweet man. I hope everything's OK."

"So do we. Can you tell us how to find him?"

"I'll have to call my supervisor for that. Wait just a moment." She picked up the white phone next to her and spoke briefly to someone. "He should be here in a few minutes."

Ashley and Steve paced. Their impatience didn't fit with Tenny's story, but she decided to let it go. The woman behind the desk was too busy to pay attention to them anyway.

Tenny saw a man approaching in the business uniform of TRANS-CAL. Before her partners could get to him, she repeated her story and asked if Thomas was working today.

"We'll have to go back to my office."

As the supervisor turned to lead the way, Tenny gave Steve a sharp elbow to the gut. He had been standing practically on top of her. "Ease up. You're going to make people suspicious."

She caught up to the supervisor and kept giving motherly glances over her shoulder to Ashley and Steve who were trying hard not to trample the poor man. The supervisor was curious about the details of their need for the information and kept asking questions as they walked. Tenny gracefully avoided further explanation, realizing that he was more interested in the police in general than the situation that had brought the three of them to him. Therefore she started to tell him a war story about one time she'd made an exciting arrest at the airport.

When they arrived at the office, the supervisor punched a few keys on the computer at his desk. "Hmm, that's unusual. Thomas changed his schedule yesterday, but he should be returning today. In fact, he's covering on a flight that should have just landed at gate thirty-nine. Here, let me call the gate and let them know that you're here to see him."

Steve was finished with deception. His huge hand came across the desk and covered the telephone. "You touch this phone and I'll arrest you for interfering with police business." The supervisor backed away from the phone and looked from one detective to the next.

As Steve and Ashley rushed out of the room, Tenny asked one more question, "What's the quickest way to get to that gate?"

Tenny sprinted out of the office past Ashley and Steve who were standing in the corridor arguing about which direction to go. As they ran through the airport, Steve was sure they were going to finally get this asshole. They had everything they needed: his identity, his location, and, most importantly, the element of surprise.

Tenny was still doubtful. This guy had gotten lucky so many times. They could use more help, but Tenny didn't want to waste valuable time explaining the situation to the Airport Police. All she wanted was every bit of strength her body could generate. She needed more speed. He couldn't be allowed to slip away again.

Ashley was nearly in tears, she was so angry. It was all her fault that it had come down to this desperate dash through the airport. She could remember how he had made her gut instinct flare when she had talked with him. Unable to keep up with her partners, Ashley cursed her ignorance and pain. If she had been healthy, she would have been the one leading the way.

▼

Steve arrived at the gate seconds before Tenny, but this time he was all business. The badge was up at eye level before he even reached the desk. "Police. Where's Thomas Whittington? He was a flight attendant on the last flight."

The flight attendant was not about to argue with the cops, especially this Terminator type. "You just missed them. They're all gone, but I didn't see him pass. He must have gone through the lower doors."

Tenny pounded the top of the check-in counter as the man cringed. "Damn it, why can't we get one damn break? When is it going to change?"

▼

The three investigators quickly huddled after their near miss at the gate and developed their next strategies. Whittington was either still at the airport or would eventually end up at his apartment. Did he know he was wanted? If he did, then infiltrating the airport with additional uniformed police officers would only make him panic and disappear. There were too many ways to sneak out of this congestion of people and vehicles. If they played it cool, they could catch him in his normal routine.

Steve left them his portable police radio and headed off to watch Whittington's house, thinking he would show up there. He wanted to be the one to catch this maniac. He was also worried about his partners. This lunatic had hurt enough women, and Steve thought it was time this asshole dealt with a man.

Tenny and Ashley were on the heels of a cooperative flight attendant leading them through the maze of airport hallways towards the employee lounge. Unable to follow the complicated directions, Tenny and Ashley were forced into the casual pace of somebody who was unaware they were hunting for a killer.

▼

Ashley quickly scanned the lounge. No luck. A woman sat near the window, the morning paper spread across the table in front of her, a cup of coffee at her elbow. "Excuse me," Tenny interrupted. "We're supposed to meet Thomas Whittington here. Have you seen him?"

The woman hardly looked up from her paper and asked, "Who's he with?"

Tenny told the woman that he had just arrived with TRANS-CAL Flight 39. "Well, I don't know him. But Cynthia has that same commuter schedule, ask her." The woman nodded towards a group seated at the counter.

"Why didn't you tell her who we are?" asked Ashley as they crossed the lounge.

"There's no point. Once you're somewhere like this, people figure that you belong here. They'll answer questions because they assume you're one of them. Why let more people know that we're looking for him?"

Ashley was awed by Tenny's thoroughness. How could she think about such details at a time like this?

"Hey, have you guys seen Thomas? He was supposed to meet me here," Tenny said, as if she were his best friend.

Cynthia eyed Ashley's battered face. "Who are you?" Tenny pulled out her badge.

Cynthia looked at Ashley again. She didn't want any part of whatever was going on. "He left about five minutes ago for the International Terminal. He's on his way to Europe for a little vacation." Cynthia said her last words to Tenny's back.

Tenny and Ashley rushed out of the lounge. Ashley was in the lead, like a bloodhound on a scent, following the signs towards the International Terminal.

Tenny grabbed Ashley by her jacket and reined her down to a walk. "Look, Ashley, we don't know how soon he's leaving or where he is between here and the terminal. Don't forget, he knows what you look like, too. If he sees you blasting through here before you see him, he'll slip away. Let's not draw attention to ourselves. Look for him everywhere."

Ashley felt her chest tighten. He could be watching her right at that moment. She spun around searching for his face, his eyes watching her, waiting for her again. She started towards the terminal, remembering the promise she had made to herself the night he had attacked her.

▼

"That's him! Oh God, it's really him." Tenny barely heard her partner's whisper. By the time she turned to look, Ashley was awkwardly drawing her gun with her left hand and struggling towards Whittington as she shouted for him to freeze.

Tenny had only moments to correct Ashley's mistake. Ashley was too far from Whittington to effect an arrest. From two hundred feet away, her confident commands only acted as a warning. As Tenny expected, the moment he heard them and saw Ashley coming towards him, he looked around for an escape route.

Tenny did the same. Here at the end of the terminal, his only way out was either past Ashley or through a door on the west side. He and Tenny sprinted towards the door. Whittington had a direct path to the door and there was no way for Ashley to cut him off. Tenny was closer, but she would have to get past several rows of chairs to reach it.

Everything around Tenny disappeared as she moved towards Whittington and the door. The airport seemed empty. She couldn't hear Ashley still screaming for him to stop and for bystanders to get out of the way. She didn't see how she maneuvered around luggage, chairs, and surprised people. All she could see was Whittington. This time, luck had to be on her side.

She hurdled the last row of chairs. Whittington hadn't been looking at Tenny as he ran, but he turned while she was in mid-flight. Their eyes met, and Tenny didn't see the fear common in fleeing suspects. She saw calm. For an instant, she even thought she saw a smile.

Whittington ducked down and away from Tenny without breaking stride, spinning as he moved forward. Tenny grabbed onto his jacket as she sailed by him. Struggling to maintain her hold, she crashed to the ground. Whittington kicked Tenny, knocking her hand away. Then he was through the door and out of sight. Tenny felt defeated. She had been so close. So many chances and everything kept going his way. It wasn't fair. It wasn't right.

Somebody ran by her through the same doorway. As it opened, the sun struck Tenny directly in the eyes, re-igniting her tenacious desire. She came off the floor like a runner coming out of the blocks and was through the doorway before the door could shut again.

She saw Ashley stumbling down a flight of stairs. Whittington was about fifty yards away, running across the pavement. Tenny pulled out the police radio as she negotiated the steps in pursuit. The radio was on, Tenny could hear routine chatter on the channel as she interrupted.

"We're in foot pursuit at the airport! We need help!" Tenny knew she was yelling over the air.

The dispatcher was professional and calm. "Please identify and repeat."

"Detective Mendoza in foot pursuit of a 187/261 suspect at the airport."

The dispatcher repeated, "10-4, all available units, we have officers in foot pursuit of a 187/261 suspect. Respond for assistance. Detective Mendoza, what is your approximate 10-20 at the airport?"

"We're entering the United hangar." Tenny gave the dispatcher their location, but the radio signal was unreadable. Every single cop within a six mile radius was on their way, but none of them knew where to go once they got to the airport.

Steve had heard Tenny's excited request over the car's radio and he knew who his friends were up against. All he could do now was get there, and hope to locate Tenny and Ashley before they cornered their prey. He pressed the accelerator to the floor.

▼

Whittington bolted through the hangar toward some surprised mechanics. One of them realized that the two women chasing the guy were police officers and tried to intercept Whittington as he passed. He only managed to slow Whittington down and get his face smashed in the process. However, it did allow Ashley and Tenny to close some distance.

Whittington was still about fifty feet ahead of the two officers when he ran through another doorway. Tenny, in the lead, followed him through the doorway and came to such an abrupt halt that Ashley almost knocked her to the ground.

They stood at one end of a long hallway. At the other end was a closed door. Between them and that door were about twenty new offices. Whittington had vanished.

Tenny moved slowly down the hall, her gun at her side. He was cornered. His luck had run out, and Tenny was ready to put an end to this hunt.

Ashley holstered her weapon. "What the hell do you think you're doing?" Ashley whispered. She grabbed Tenny's arm and backed out of the hallway. "We're not going down this hall without backup. Give me the radio." Ashley dragged her partner back to the door.

Tenny spun around, her face so taut that Ashley thought a simple touch would shatter it. "Look, this damn radio isn't even transmitting out of this fucking area, or we would already have backup. I'm not leaving here without him, and there are no phones except possibly in those offices, and that's where he's waiting." She pointed defiantly down the hall.

Ashley was confused. Her training told her to keep the hall under surveillance and wait for backup. Yet she was feeling all the same emotions as Tenny, plus one other: she was frightened.

As if Tenny had read Ashley's mind, her expression relaxed, but the confidence remained. She reached out and touched Ashley's face. "You're not alone this time. I'm here, and together we can end this."

Ashley reminded herself that she had taken many assholes to jail, and this one was no different. She trusted Tenny as she had never trusted a partner before.

"OK," she said, "but we are going to do this right. First, turn off that damn radio so we move in silence. Use only hand signals and keep your back to the wall. I only have one good hand, so I'll go first and cover you as you try the doors. Here's a pocket mirror. Don't make an entry until you check the room. Any questions?" Ashley removed a small mirror from the back of her badge holder.

"None." Tenny was impressed. She had never seen Ashley take control like this before.

Ashley brought her left arm and her weapon into a ready position and started towards the first door with Tenny following. Tenny was focused on the door with her weapon pointed towards the floor, ready to snap it up in a second. If that door knob moved a fraction, Tenny would see it.

When they reached the door, Ashley stepped across the hall and positioned herself between Tenny and the remainder of the hallway. Without taking her eyes from down the hall, she motioned with her cast for Tenny to try the door. For a second, neither of them breathed. Tenny reached out slowly and touched the doorknob. She turned, wondering what would happen next.

Locked!

Tenny was about to relax when suddenly Whittington's voice came from behind them. "Hey, you two stupid dyke cops, are you ready to get fucked by a man?"

Ashley felt the swell of panic start in her stomach and rush towards her head. Tenny, jerking around to defend herself, saw a speaker on the wall. She touched Ashley's arm and pointed upward.

"Pick up your nearest white courtesy phone and I'll tell you all about the rest of the cunts I straightened out and how I'm going to do the same to you bitches."

Whittington had found a telephone and was on the airport public announcement system taunting them, trying to fluster them, in a desperate attempt to swing luck back in his favor. It wasn't going to work this time. They remained courageously calm under the rain of insults and challenges hurled at them. Tenny moved cautiously towards the next door as Ashley held her position to cover the locked one.

▼

"What the fuck do you mean, you can't tell me where it's coming from?" Steve was losing his temper. The chafing voice of this lunatic was driving him crazy. "Then shut him off!"

"We can't do that either without bringing down the whole system, and I don't know how," the airport official said helplessly.

The entire airport was in a frenzy. Airport officials were shocked and dismayed, not knowing how to stop the ugly viciousness. The police paced like trained fighting dogs waiting to be let loose. Passengers were trying to escape from the voice. Everybody could sense the danger and guessed that somebody was about to get hurt.

Steve, who knew exactly what was occurring, felt paralyzed. His partners had Whittington cornered somewhere in this mass of confusion, and this time the lunatic wouldn't run. This time it was all or nothing, and three lives were on the line.

An airport officer, standing next to Steve, heard the radio dispatcher. "Attention all officers, a mechanic reports seeing two officers chasing a male through the United hangar about five minutes ago. We are still unable to raise the detectives." Airport officers began to run down the corridor, with the city police and Steve right behind them.

"Please let it be all right," Steve prayed with a knot in his stomach and a lump in his throat. "We're coming, we're coming."

Tenny reached slowly for the door knob of the next office. It was hard to concentrate on the door with the obscenities raining down on them from the speaker. His tone was so dangerous, so savage, almost inhuman. She turned the knob: unlocked.

The last three offices had all been unlocked. They had taken the chance of creating a crossfire when she had moved past the first unlocked office, but there was no safe alternative. Now they had established a pattern, and when she gave Ashley the unlocked signal, Ashley waved her back to the first office.

Tenny came back and stood next to Ashley. They spoke to each other in normal voices in order to be heard over Whittington's taunts. Ashley's eyes never left the door and Tenny's continued to scan the hall.

Ashley gave the commands. "I'll take a low position on the left side. You kick the door and then take a high position behind me. Here, give me the mirror, I can use my right hand to check the room." Ashley started to crouch into her position and then stood once again. The anxiety was unmistakable in her voice. "I know he's in this office. I can feel him."

"I know," Tenny reassured her. "We're going to end it right now, together." Ashley kneeled on the left side of the door with her gun pointing directly towards the door. When it came flying open, she would be ready.

Tenny took a moment to plan her strategy. She would have to take her eyes off the hall for a moment in order to kick the door. Then she would spin into the wall next to Ashley and resume her watch of the hall. If he was setting them up, preparing to spring from another office, she would be ready for him. She reminded herself to kick next to the doorknob to get it on the first try. Then she launched into action.

The door burst open easily with the impact of her kick. The voice on the speaker stopped. The phone receiver hit the floor. Ashley heard Whittington moving inside the office, and Tenny heard the same over the speaker system. Then there was silence.

▼

The entire airport heard the office door explode and the phone drop. Everybody stopped to hear what would come next, captured in place by the intensity of the moment and by the realization that they would hear the end.

Steve grabbed the airport officer's arm. "How close are we?" The officer pointed to a hangar just outside the window.

"That's it."

Steve dreaded hearing it all happen over the open speaker system. He forced himself on.

Ashley tried to raise the mirror, but her swollen hand was shaking badly in its heavy cast. Ashley was becoming angry. Again, she felt Tenny's hand on her shoulder, firm and comforting. This time it would be different.

The mirror came up and Ashley slowly moved it into the doorway to scan the office. She was searching for another door. If Whittington was trapped, she would make Tenny pull back and wait for additional officers. There was no safe way to enter the office, and no reason to take the risk if he really couldn't run anymore.

Tenny watched the hallway and the left side of the office. Whittington was nowhere in sight, but the largest portion of the room was behind the wall that shielded them.

Tenny had been surprised at how easily the door had flown open, but now she understood why. The inside of the office was still under construction and only the outside wall was in place. Tenny realized with a shudder that only a half-inch piece of drywall stood between her and Whittington.

She felt Ashley's shoulder tense. In the small mirror all they could see were a pair of legs creeping along on the inside of the wall towards the door. Ashley adjusted the mirror upwards.

"Ax! He's got an ax!"

Tenny glanced back towards the door they had first come through. Next to it was a glass emergency fire box. It had everything: an alarm, a hose, even a place for the ax. Why hadn't she noticed earlier?

"Shit!" Tenny had only seconds left. Ashley was in a horrible position. The only way she could get a shot off would be to cross the doorway, becoming an easy target. Tenny did not have a shot either. As soon as Whittington reached the doorway, he would be swinging the ax at Ashley, and they would only have a moment to drop him. Even if both Tenny and Ashley were able to hit him, their bullets might not be enough to stop the deadly motion of the ax. They were caught without an appropriate plan.

Tenny grabbed Ashley's shoulder. Pulling her back and down, away from the door and wall, Tenny fired eight of her fifteen rounds, back and forth, high and low, in a three-foot section of the drywall. After the burst of gunfire, both detectives kneeled and aimed at the office door. They waited.

▼

Steve was racing desperately towards the new offices, not daring to think about what he was hearing over the still-open PA system. He didn't even pause at the sound of Ashley's voice screaming her warning. The shots that followed ripped into Steve's soul as he reached the door to the hallway.

20

The door opened at the far end of the hallway. Ashley swung her gun around to confront any threat. Recognizing Steve, she swung back to the office door, communicating to Steve where the real danger lay.

Steve rushed up with his own weapon drawn, relieved to see his partners still untouched. Reaching the door, he waved Ashley's and Tenny's guns down and brought up his own, arms locked in front of him. Steve could see a pool of blood just inside the room and thought that the suspect must have collapsed out of sight. He listened for moans or labored breathing. Hearing nothing, he started into the room.

"What are you doing?" hissed Ashley.

"He's dead." Steve knew they couldn't see the blood. He stepped into the room to find the corpse, his gun dropped to his side, his body slacking-off with his mind.

"Shit." In a flash Steve knew he had made an awful mistake.

Whittington was standing right in front of Steve. All Steve could see was the person, then the blood, then the smile on Whittington's face. Steve's gun was coming into a firing position, but out of the corner of his eye, Steve caught a gleam of an ax swinging through the air at head level from his left.

Before Steve could comprehend the danger he was in, his left arm instinctively came up, his hand catching the ax fractions of a moment before impact, saving his life. The momentum of the wild swing still bit deep into Steve's left shoulder, throwing his body into the wall. His right arm and his gun were pinned momentarily.

Ashley and Tenny heard Steve's angry cry of pain, but neither could see what was happening inside the office. Ashley slid across the doorway, but all she could see was Steve leaning against the wall. She knew Whittington was standing on the other side. She had a kill shot if Steve would get out of the way.

"Steve, down! Down!" Ashley screamed furiously.

She saw the ax coming around, preparing for another fatal swing at Steve's head. But he was not concentrating on police tactics. His mind had switched into a pure survival mode and was shutting out external distractions.

"Get down! Get down!" Instead, Steve was trying to push away from the wall and free his own weapon to protect himself.

Ashley looked to Tenny for help. Tenny had her gun leveled once again at the wall, glaring in concentration. Ashley knew that Tenny couldn't see their positions in the room and, therefore, couldn't shoot.

Ashley screamed, "Shoot right! Shoot right!"

The rounds exploded through the wall as the ax began its deadly course. Pieces of the wall burst around Whittington in a sudden shower. He staggered back, the ax swinging helplessly short of Steve's body. Blinded by the particles blasting from the wall, Steve brought up his gun and fired. All his efforts were focused on reacting, and Steve still didn't hear Ashley's adament orders to fall to the floor.

A sharp pain in his right hand forced his gun from his grasp. Then a blunt force rammed into his gut. Steve grabbed the object and forced his eyes open. Whittington stood there. None of the shots had struck him.

Steve twisted Whittington's ax away and threw it down. Reaching for the man that had hurt his friend, he discovered that he had little strength in either his left arm or his right hand. Whittington easily deflected Steve's lunge and then thrust his own body towards Steve's knees. The force of the collision sent both men back into the doorway and to the ground.

Through the pain Steve heard Ashley and Tenny yelling for him to get clear. His partners would have a shot if he could just break free. Twisting from side to side, Steve used all the strength he had to stand.

Whittington was still clinging to Steve as they lurched into the hallway. Tenny leapt from her position to avoid being crushed. Both men crashed against the wall, bounced off and ended up in the middle of the hall still gripping one another. The pain was paralyzing, but Steve managed to bring his arms up and pushed.

Whittington went flying through the air and landed a good ten feet down the hall. Steve stood waiting for the burst of shots that would end all this.

There was nothing. Whittington scrambled to his feet and turned to run. Steve was confused and disoriented. Where were his partners? Two guns met his face as he spun around. He was directly in their line of fire.

"Shit!" Steve dropped to the floor and heard the gunfire above him. Feet nicked his broken body and ran down the hall-way. He pushed himself from the floor to join the pursuit. His injuries were bad, but nothing would be as bad as giving up.

Tenny couldn't believe it. While Steve stood as his protection, Whittington had fled down the hall. Their shots had been deflected by the closing door. Yet as she set into pursuit, Tenny knew that this couldn't last long. There had to be dozens of officers closing in on them right now. There was no way for the suspect to escape.

Moving slowly and cautiously, they followed a trail of blood through the maze of offices. The entire airport had to be crawling with cops. He was bound to run into a few, and the blood covering him was the only information an officer needed to take him into custody. But, as they reached the staircase leading up to the main terminal area, a terrible apprehension seized Tenny.

"Ashley, something's wrong. Where is everybody? There's no help."

Ashley couldn't answer. They reached the top of the stairs, pushed open the door, and stepped into the terminal.

▼

Everybody in the airport had been frozen in place as they heard the hunt over the PA system. But when the sound of gunfire blasted through the speakers, panic had turned into hysteria. One person running for the exits was all it took to transform orderly routine into a deadly stampede. The police officers forgot about the chase. Attempting to restore calm and prevent catastrophic chaos became their priority. Their efforts were futile.

Tenny could not believe her eyes. Thousands of bodies were pushing, shoving, forcing their way towards exits which could only accommodate a few at a time. Officers were yelling at people to be calm, but the repeated gunshots had fed the hysteria. People were being crushed. Screaming, yelling, and crying fueled the swell of panic.

At last Steve stumbled through the door. "Oh my God," he gasped.

Tenny regained her composure. "He's in there somewhere."

All three detectives scanned the crowd. Tenny started her search towards the rear of the crowd and worked forward towards the exits. Frightened people at the rear of the mob added their confusion and fear.

"There! There!" Ashley screamed, pointing over the crowd. Whittington inched forward, trying to stay on his feet, moving towards freedom. Ashley dove into the crowd behind Steve, who was desperately trying to act as battering ram, pushing his way through the crowd. Nobody wanted to give up any of their progress. Everybody was so focused on their own escape that they didn't respond to Ashley waving her badge or Steve's blood-soaked shirt.

Tenny leaped up onto a ticket counter, trying to draw attention to herself and point out the suspect to the officers clinging to the exits. Steve and Ashley would never be able to reach Whittington before he disappeared into the scattering crowd outside the exit. The officers at the doors were the only hope, but the noise of the fleeing crowd drowned her shouts.

Tenny grabbed the radio still clipped onto her belt. "Code-three traffic! Code-three traffic!"

An alert dispatcher jumped in to assist. "All units hold your traffic for code-three traffic. Units hold your traffic!" Both of their efforts seemed to fall on deaf ears as officers continued their disjointed communications over the air.

Code-three traffic could be an officer whose life was endangered. A long, high-pitched tone blasted from Tenny's radio and was followed by the dispatcher's angry voice. "Units hold your traffic! Hold your traffic for code-three traffic." Silence followed. "Unit with code-three traffic go ahead."

"This is Detective Mendoza. I'm in the main terminal at the exits. The 187 suspect is attempting to flee through the exits with the crowd. Stand by for location."

Tenny had taken her eyes off Whittington. Now she could not find him again. Her heart raced with anxiety as she scanned the area where she had last seen him. Nothing. He had disappeared.

Tenny heard the dispatcher asking for the location, and Steve's voice screaming her name. She saw him in the crowd, his bloody right hand motioning ahead and to his left. Tenny followed its invisible path and spotted Whittington.

"He's almost to exit six! Exit six!"

The officer at the exit had been clutching the handle of the door to avoid being swept away. Tenny could see that Whittington would pass directly out the middle of the exit. The officer pushed and yelled at the crowd in an effort to reach him, but the crush of bodies was unyielding and both he and Tenny realized that the suspect would pass through the doors just out of the officer's reach. Finally, he drew his weapon. At the sight of the gun, the crowd in exit six surged forward, carrying Whittington with them.

▼

Just before the surge, Whittington looked back, locked his gaze with Tenny's, and smiled at her apparent helplessness to stop him and his impending escape. Tenny couldn't believe it. The bastard was smiling. He had won and now he was taunting her again. She had failed to capture him. She couldn't stop him. It was over.

Then Tenny had an idea, a last chance. She extended her right hand and slowly curled down three fingers and gave him the international sign of disrespect. She flipped him off. The smile vanished from Whittington's face. The last thing Tenny saw as he was swept through the doors was the look of pure rage. The challenge had been accepted.

Except for Ashley and Steve, Tenny didn't recognize anyone in the crowded room. Steve looked uncomfortable, both from his injuries and from the amount of brass milling about. Spotting Tenny, he smiled and nudged Ashley, who looked over and gave Tenny a wink and her fabulous smile.

The investigators had not seen each other since the incident at the airport. They had all been placed on restricted duty while the departments conducted a joint internal investigation of the shooting, how Steve had sustained his injuries, and most importantly, what had caused the wave of panic which had left several people seriously injured and many others suffering minor injuries. Yesterday Tenny, Ashley, and Steve had been cleared of any wrongful acts.

During the last two weeks, Ashley and Tenny had supervised volunteers staffing tip phones in their respective departments. Immediately after Whittington's escape, the two Chiefs of Police decided to make this investigation public. Whittington's name and a full description were released to the press, along with a synopsis of all the crimes he had allegedly committed over the last several months. The true link among the victims was not divulged. Instead, the media was led to believe that the only thing the women had in common were the cities where they lived.

Tenny followed her Captain and Chief over to several empty seats and sat down as they moved towards the coffee. She noticed Margo seated directly across the room from her and discreetly away from Ashley. Margo smiled at Tenny and then gently mouthed the words, "I'm sorry." Tenny returned the smile and nodded her head.

"Well, if it isn't Detective 'Tenacity' Mendoza!" Diane Barker was standing in front of her. Tenny had not returned any of her phone calls. Now Tenny was cornered and she was expected to be cooperative with the press.

She tried to be polite. "Yes, I was one of the primary investigators in this case." Tenny shot a look in Ashley's direction hoping to obtain backup, but Ashley was busy with Tenny's Chief. Steve caught her distress signal from across the room.

"I still want to know why a homicide detective was assigned to a serial rapist investigation."

"It's not only a—"

"I needed her expertise on my investigation." Steve to the rescue. "Hi. I'm Steve Carson. I was the head detective on this investigation," he said, effectively preventing Tenny from announcing that it was a homicide investigation now. The departments were not releasing that information.

"Oh?" said Barker, annoyed. "Well, what was your role Detective Mendoza?" She wasn't going to let Mendoza slip out of this conversation.

Before Barker even had the question completed, Steve was answering. "All the detectives in this case acted as equals...." As Steve launched into his lengthy, but useless, description of their investigation, he stepped slightly between Barker and Tenny. Tenny started to walk away.

Both detectives were surprised when Barker reached around

Steve and touched Tenny's arm, knowing better than to grab a cop.

"I want to speak with you, Detective. In fact, I've been trying to get an interview with the great Detective Tenacity for quite some time. Your involvement in this case would make a perfect excuse to do a story on you."

Steve quickly glanced over his shoulder at Tenny and recognized the look of the 'ice woman'. This encounter was going downhill fast. Steve looked towards Ashley for additional backup, but she was surrounded by the brass of both departments and had her back to Steve.

Tenny started to say something in a voice as hard and sharp as sleet, but Steve jumped in. "Why do you want a story on her? She's boring. Anyway, the story of this case has been told so many times that I think everybody is sick of it."

"Detective, you and I both know that the bullshit that has been passed out to the media is nothing. I want to know why Detective Mendoza and Detective Johnson were assigned to the case. I want to know how the suspect was identified. I want to know why you attempted an arrest at a crowded airport. I want to know about the mysterious Tenacity that never speaks to reporters. And if she doesn't want to set an appointment with me, then I'll go speak to her Chief!"

Margo approached, and Tenny knew that she would be able to get this reporter away from her, but Tenny was too angry to care. "I don't talk to reporters because I don't like them, and I don't like you. I could give a shit if my Chief orders me to talk to you. It won't happen!" Tenny turned and walked off, just as Margo arrived. This Barker woman was not going to go away.

▼

"OK, folks, let's get started." Ashley's Chief stepped to the center of the room. "I've invited all of you here because we need to discuss how much longer we are going to continue our efforts to apprehend this suspect, Thomas Whittington.

Members of the press are here because we feel that you all have become law enforcement's partners in this case."

Diane Barker interrupted. "Chief, if we're partners, then why is it that you haven't shared the truth with us about why an arrest attempt of a known, dangerous felon was made at a crowded airport?"

The Chief looked at his press officer, who had promised him that this wouldn't happen. The press officer immediately moved to shelter his Chief and save his career.

"Diane, as I explained to you and your producer, this is not a press conference. Those have already occurred. This meeting's sole purpose is to decide what to do next."

Another reporter recognized that Diane had hit on something. "I see this as more of a chance to try and get the media to buy any decision you have already made, and that's not going to happen if all the facts of the case haven't been revealed."

The press officer turned to look at Tenny. He had observed her run-in with Diane and felt he had Tenny to thank for this disaster in the making.

"Now, that's not true. No decisions have been made yet. We want to move on. The relevant facts in this case have been shared with the media, including the fact that an internal investigation was performed on the incident at the airport and it revealed that the investigating detectives did nothing wrong. In fact, they risked their lives in a heroic effort to apprehend the suspect." The Chief was trying to defuse the situation, but Barker had decided earlier that she was going to get this story no matter what it took.

"I'm sorry, Chief, but none of the press releases or press conferences explained why the arrest was attempted at the airport, and I think that's something people have a right to know."

Margo was growing angry. She knew that both departments were simply trying to protect Ashley from the media. Like all the other victims, her name and the specifics of her attack had not been made public. Yet her attack was the key to the suspect identification. Her loss of memory was what had led to the situation at the airport. Margo glanced across the room and noticed Tenny whispering to a woman from a victim advocacy group. Tenny had moved to a different seat when the discussion had begun and now Margo could guess why. She had noticed that fear, embarrassment, and pain were already beginning to show on Ashley's face.

Finally the victim advocate stood up. "Look, I've had enough of this bickering! I'm not here to rehash what has already happened, and I'm one of the people you think have a right to know." She glared at Barker. "I'm here to make sure that this maniac never hurts anybody again and that everything is being done to catch him. I resent your interference in achieving this goal and I don't like your accusatory manner. For once the police are letting us participate in their decision-making process. They don't have to, and you're spoiling it! If you don't want to participate in the discussion which we are all here to have, then you should leave!"

Margo leaned back in her chair and smiled at Tenny. None of the media representatives wanted to take on the public themselves.

The group discussed the follow-up investigation of the past two weeks. Most of the experts believed that Whittington had fled into Mexico, where he most likely died from his injuries. All had agreed that the investigation would be considered inactive at this time, but if any additional information was discovered the team of investigators would immediately be brought together again to follow up on it.

Several people noticed that Detective Mendoza had not offered any thoughts on what had happened to the suspect. In fact, during the entire discussion she hadn't said a word even when prompted slightly by her Captain. Tenny had sat quietly in the room, obviously miles away in thought. Ashley was concerned that Tenny was once again burdening herself with responsibility for his escape. Diane Barker was convinced that Tenny was not sharing everything she knew, and she was determined to discover what she was hiding.

▼

The three friends left the meeting quickly. None of them wanted to be cornered by a boss, a reporter, or anybody else. All they wanted was time to themselves.

Tenny pulled the rental car into the public parking at the beach, got out, and walked back towards the street. Steve was about to ask her what she was doing when he felt Ashley pulling on his sleeve.

"Come on, let's go get some good seats. She'll be back."

"Some good seats? What are you talking about?" Steve looked confused. "It's a huge beach and there's not another soul within a hundred yards."

"Come on." Ashley dragged Steve out onto the beach and right down to the edge of the dry sand. Then they sat. "Best seats in the house," Ashley announced proudly.

Tenny returned within minutes and sat down between them. She had a bottle of wine and plastic champagne glasses. Ashley smiled.

Tenny turned to her. "These are great seats, good job. I taught you well," said Tenny.

Steve welcomed the fresh air and the relaxing warmth of the sand. Watching the waves roll gently in, he wondered how far they had traveled. Tenny handed Ashley and Steve a glass of wine and they raised them in a toast. "Here's to putting an end to a little piece of hate that exists in the world."

Ashley looked at Steve and Tenny. "I'm glad that I had the chance to meet both of you and I hope our friendship lasts as long as the sand on which we are seated." They took a sip of their wine and looked back to the ocean.

Moments later Steve, grimacing with effort, once again lifted his glass. "Here's to two women whose courage, strength, and love not only stopped an insane human, but also taught an unwilling student to really accept people for who they are and not what I think they should be. You two never used my own anger and ignorance against me. You never allowed my hostility to create the same in you. I'll never be able to explain to you the feeling I had when I thought that you two were being hurt. But when I saw you both all right, I almost started to cry, and I knew that we would be friends and partners for life. Both of you will always be able to count on me."

Once again they raised their glasses in a toast, and both Steve and Ashley were on the verge of tears. It was Tenny's turn.

"Here's to the ocean, the sand, the wind, and the sky. No matter how hard things get, they serve as constant reminders of the immensity of life. I'm just glad we're all alive to enjoy them now."

They sat in silence for a while. Finally, Ashley asked, "Steve, are you all right?"

Steve looked in her direction with a set jaw. "I'm fine." He fingered the sand nervously.

Tenny encouraged him. "Remember what you said a few minutes ago about being there for us? Well, would you please let us to do the same for you?"

Steve looked down at the sand and dropped his left hand to it. He tried to grab a handful, but his hand would not respond to his mind's commands. He looked to his right hand, encased in a splint that barely allowed him to grasp the wine glass. He knew his career was over.

"I suffered extensive nerve damage to my left arm as well as muscle and tendon destruction. The doctors expect about thirty to forty percent recovery with physical therapy. I should have almost full recovery in my right hand, although things like writing will be much more difficult."

Steve caught his breath, a lump stuck in his throat. He didn't know how to continue. Not now nor with his life. He looked at

Tenny and she took his left hand in her hands and lifted his helpless arm to her knee.

The pain slipped into his voice. "I've never been anything but a cop. I never wanted to do anything else. It's more than a job to me. It's a part of who I am, what I believe in. It's part of my heart." He looked at Tenny and Ashley and with the lump of truth which choked his words came his tears. "I'll never be a cop again."

Ashley spoke through her own clenched teeth. "Damn it, Steve! You'll always be a cop. You may not be in the job, but what we do is more than that. You'll always carry that special power with you. That ability which makes us able to do what we do, when others can't. It's caring enough to put it all on the line for strangers and what you believe in. You carry that inside you, Steve. You said so yourself. That's what will always make you a cop. That's what sets us apart!"

Both Tenny and Steve nodded as Ashley spoke. Her words were so true, but something that most cops rarely shared. Tenny was proud of Ashley for saying it, and she was proud of Steve for trusting them.

Tenny grabbed Ashley's hand and brought it to Steve's and her own. "We're all going to get through this together and put an end to this asshole's destruction once and for all." She vowed to herself that the next time Thomas Whittington and she came face to face—she would end it.

22

Tenny pushed back from her desk and stood slowly. She had been so absorbed by her task that she had ignored the small signals her body had been providing. Now pain sprang from her neck to her toes. The police information had been interesting but inconsequential to Tenny's search. After Whittington had escaped from the airport, the only thing that anybody could concentrate on was locating him. The information in the reports reflected this priority.

This was not what interested Tenny. She needed to know why. Why was he attacking only lesbians? Why was he saying the things that he did? Why had he killed his last victim? Tenny had made a list of his friends and family. Tomorrow she would start speaking with each of them.

She put the names in her drawer and was on her way out of the office when the phone rang. "Homicide. Detective Mendoza speaking."

"Hey, girl, what's happening?" Ashley's voice was filled with happiness and all of Tenny's apprehension and concern evaporated.

Tenny couldn't help but smile. "What're you so happy about?"

"I tell you, I'm starting to believe in fate and all that stuff. If Steve wasn't so delirious with relief he would be calling you himself, but he got swept away by a bunch of happy officers for a major celebration. Hey, why don't you fly down here and join us?"

"You haven't told me what I'm celebrating yet." Tenny was wondering if Steve had won the lottery.

"Steve got promoted to Sergeant."

"What? That's impossible, he's retiring out due to his injuries."

"No such luck." Ashley was overflowing with joy.

"Tell me what's going on." Tenny was laughing too, but she still didn't understand why.

"He got promoted to Sergeant since he was next on the list anyway. There's a special training position which was going to be implemented in the next fiscal year, but the city council and mayor decided to move it up. They created the position immediately and put Steve in it. He's in charge of a new community-police training program. Now is that fate, or what?"

"So he's still a cop?"

"Yep. I guess under the Americans with Disabilities Act the city created a new classification for officers disabled on the job and he retains full benefits and peace officer status, but he can't return to a position requiring arrest powers. It's weird, but the important thing is that he's still a cop and he's staying with us."

Tenny was doing a small victory dance in her office as she shouted, "Yes, yes, yes!"

"Pretty amazing, eh? You should have seen Steve's face when they told him, it was great. So, you coming down?"

"I can't, but you tell that big lug to call me when he comes down off of cloud nine."

"OK, I'll talk to you soon. Take care." Ashley hung up.

Tenny was so excited that she ran up and down the hall

trying to find someone to tell. She wanted to celebrate. She wanted to scream for joy. She wanted to hug Steve.

Instead, she went back to her office and once again packed up to go home.

The phone rang again. "Tenny, can you stop by my office on your way out please?"

When the Captain wanted to speak to her, Tenny made herself available. "Sure. I'll be right there."

▼

"Come in, Tenny." The Captain waved her into his office and towards a chair as soon as she appeared outside his door.

"How are you doing? I haven't really had a chance to talk to you since the whole thing at the airport. At least not on a more personal level." The Captain had made an effort to keep Tenny informed of the progress and findings of the internal investigation.

"I'm doing pretty good, although I can't help wishing things had come out differently."

"Yeah, don't you worry about that. Everybody around here knows that you did everything you could to get that asshole."

The words "everything you could" made Tenny wince. She thought of Pearl.

The Captain continued, "I think you need to get back to your normal routine as quickly as possible. I would be happy to give you some time off if you'd like, and then I want to get you back into Homicide."

"I think the restricted duty during the internal was enough time off. But I'm not done with this investigation yet, Captain." Tenny tried to look nonchalant.

"I'm not sure I know what you're talking about. The investigation has been placed in the inactive files. The suspect is assumed to have fled the country. He may be dead. What's left to do?"

Tenny saw that the Captain, like everybody else that had been involved in this case, was simply glad it was over. That was enough for him. It would never be enough for Tenny.

"Captain, we both know that just because the case is inactive, it's not closed. It doesn't just go away. I want to know why this idiot was hurting lesbians. I think I owe it to the victims to find out." Her voice and eyes were intense.

The Captain met Tenny's stare. For a moment he remembered what it was like to be in her place. To be asked why over and over. He should have known Tenny wouldn't walk away from it at this point. Not with a chance to find the answer.

"Is two weeks enough?"

Tenny smiled slightly and nodded in thanks. "That'll be plenty." She stood to leave.

"One more thing. What's going on with this reporter, Barker?"

Tenny sunk back into her chair. Obviously Diane Barker had made good on her threat. "Why? What did she do?"

"She called and insisted that you were being uncooperative and wanted me to order you to provide her with an interview regarding the rape investigation."

Tenny grimaced. "I can't talk to her. She's trying to dig up some dirt and turn his attacks into a sensational story. I'm not going to help her do that."

The Captain said patronizingly, "Tenny, it has always been my experience that if you cooperate with the media things turn out much better than if you don't. I think that if you handle her right, you can give her enough information to make her happy and still not give up anything really important. Just steer her in the direction you want her to go."

Tenny shook her head. "I don't think that'll work with this newshound. She's already digging for information that would lead her right to Ashley. I'm not going to talk to Barker."

The Captain leaned forward. "What if I ordered you to?"

"Then it would be time for me to look for a new job."

He smiled, knowing that Tenny would call his bluff. "I guess I'll have to take care of her myself then."

"That's what you get the big bucks for." Tenny laughed as she walked out of the office.

▼

Leaning casually against the huge Chevy Suburban which was the mobile television unit, Diane Barker sipped her tea to fend off the chill of the morning air. Shadowing Mendoza would make for a long and challenging day. She tapped the side of her mug in annoyance. Cops always managed to protect each other.

Diane knew there was a story behind this investigation. Her reporter instincts had been screaming at her ever since she revealed the makeup of the team investigating the serial rapes. It wasn't every day that a female rookie was pulled from patrol and assigned to a major, multiple-agency investigation. Then on top of that, another department pulls their top female investigator out of homicide and puts her on the joint investigation. Why?

The departments had done an impressive job of keeping this investigation out of the media. Though Diane had requested records on all the rapes during the last four months, she knew that the names and addresses of the victims would be deleted. She couldn't even be sure how long ago the rapes had started. Therefore, nobody knew exactly how many victims there had been. Nobody knew the sequence of attacks. Nobody knew the motive. Everybody knew the suspect.

And they expected Diane to be satisfied with their theorizing that the suspect had fled the country or died: end of story. Well, Diane wasn't about to let this investigation go away quietly. She wanted the truth even if she had to follow this Tenacity woman for weeks.

▼

"Shit!" Tenny's morning had gotten off to a bad start. There was Barker, right at the entrance of the employee parking lot as Tenny pulled into work. She shot past the television vehicle and drove all the way to the opposite end of the lot. She jumped from her car quickly and headed for the holding area door at a fast walk.

Tenny glanced back towards the parking lot entrance and saw Barker running through a restricted area to intercept her. Tenny was angered by Barker's arrogance, but she didn't want a confrontation, especially with this reporter. She fought the urge to sprint for the door, forcing herself to slow her pace and keep Barker waiting for a few seconds.

Diane watched as the detective strode confidently over the cold asphalt. She had found Mendoza attractive since the first time she had seen her years ago. She enjoyed the woman's aloofness and her magical way of controlling situations without appearing in control. Although Tenacity's abilities had often made her reporting more difficult, Diane couldn't help but respect this woman. It was too bad she was a cop.

"Good morning, Detective. If you don't mind, I have a few questions for you."

Tenny stopped directly in front of the reporter and glared. Diane felt those eyes burn right through her.

"I do mind. In fact, I mind that you even are standing in my path this morning."

Tenny moved to go around Barker, but the reporter blocked her. Tenny shot into a police-ready stance, surprised that somebody had actually prevented her from having the last word.

"Whoa, you're not going to hurt me, are you, Detective?" Diane tried to hide her fear with sarcastic humor. Tenny said nothing, she simply gave Barker a look which she simultaneously found intimidating and exciting. "I don't understand why you're being so evasive. What are you trying to hide?" Diane sounded almost apologetic.

"I don't understand why you're being so insistent. I told you that there's no story here. Why don't you go dig around in somebody else's business? This city is full of juicy stories. You're wasting your time with this investigation which is done and gone." There was no mistaking Tenny's anger.

"If that's true, why won't you talk to me?"

"There's nothing to talk about."

"I think you're wrong, and I intend to follow you everywhere until I know what you know."

Tenny had had enough. She placed her hand on Barker's arm and gave her a firm push to the side as Tenny stepped by her and opened the door. "You do what you want, but you'll miss all the real stories."

Tenny barely heard Barker squeeze the last words through the closing door.

"I think I've already found it."

▼

"Margo, this reporter is going to drive me crazy. Isn't there any way I can legally get her off my case?"

Tenny had marched directly up to her office and managed to catch Margo before she left her office for the courtroom. As the media liaison for the District Attorney, Margo was an expert at dealing with the press.

"Look, Tenny, I checked into this Barker gal because I'm worried about Ashley. You better watch yourself around her. Apparently Diane Barker has a pretty impressive reputation of her own. She always seems to get her story one way or another, and there's nothing you can do legally to keep her away."

"Shit! What do I do? You're not telling me to just give her everything, are you?"

"No, no way! The confidentiality law is still on your side. But we both know if she keeps looking, eventually she will find somebody that'll talk. We've only been lucky so far. Maybe you should give her something. Try giving her enough to set her off in the wrong direction."

Tenny sighed. She was starting to feel a little defeated. "I've already risked that once. If she finds out I sent her on a wild goose hunt, do you think she'll ever forget this whole thing?"

"No, but maybe by the time she figures it out, her producer will be tired of this game, or a bigger story will break. You need to try, Tenny." Tenny could hear the worry in Margo's voice.

"Hey, don't worry. If worse comes to worst, I'll enrage her to the point that she writes a stinging article about me. It wouldn't be the first time.

"Give me a call, and let me know what happens. I might be able to help. I know some people in the business up there that owe me a favor or two."

"You got it. Thanks for the information, Margo, and make sure you make the cops look good on the stand today."

"Oh, so now you're asking for miracles, huh?" Margo and Tenny both laughed.

Tenny hung up and walked downstairs to the briefing room. She leaned against the doorway as the Lieutenant finished reading an interdepartmental memo to the troops. He looked up and spotted her. "So what brings the traveling Detective Tenacity to our briefing? You haven't been solving our murders, so you couldn't be here to chew out my officers for screwing up one of your crime scenes."

Tenny smiled and shook her head. The Lieutenant was right. She usually only came down to a patrol briefing when somebody had made a stupid and costly mistake at a crime scene or during an investigation.

"No problems today, LT, just visiting."

"Bullshit! What do you want?"

"Well, if you could spare one of your fine officers, I could use a marked unit for about fifteen minutes to help me with a persistent reporter."

All the officers in the room sat up straight in anticipation of a chance to mess with the press a little. The Lieutenant smiled and shook a finger at Tenny. "Now, now, we all know that the media representatives are our friends. If we treat them with respect and dignity, then they will return that consideration." The Lieutenant looked out into the briefing room. "Lee, will you be kind enough to assist Detective Mendoza with removing that Barker woman from her ass?"

"I guess she's still out there." Tenny indicated the holding entrance, which almost all the officers used to enter the building.

Lee was a skinny, boyish-looking officer with about two years on, but he had already developed a dislike for the press. "She's out there all right, asking everybody to bring her in and get her a pass."

"Great! Lee, come up to my office when you're ready to go into service." Tenny waved and returned to her work.

▼

As soon as Tenny pulled out of the parking lot in her unmarked vehicle, the Suburban almost rammed her as the driver gunned to get into traffic right behind. Lee, in his marked patrol car, melted cooly into traffic behind the Suburban as all the surrounding drivers went out of their way to yield to the police car.

Barker's cameraman got an uneasy feeling as soon as he saw the patrol car pull in behind him. "I don't think we're going to get far, Diane," he said, pointing to the rearview mirror.

She looked over her shoulder and waved to the officer, but got no response. "He can't do anything to us if we don't do anything wrong. Just stay with her."

About five blocks later the caravan stopped at a red light. Tenny waited a few seconds, then calmly pulled down the red emergency light in her windshield. Suddenly the morning was filled with the screech of Tenny's siren.

"She can't do this." Diane knew exactly what was about to happen.

"I think she can, and I know she's about to." The cameraman knew defeat when he saw it.

Tenny waited for all the cross traffic to realize that her Cherokee was actually a police vehicle. Then she floored her car through the intersection and disappeared around the corner.

"Follow her, damn it! Come on!" Diane pounded the dashboard.

Forgetting the patrol car directly behind him, the cameraman burst through the red light in pursuit of Tenny. He barely made it to the other side of the intersection before Lee's own siren and red light were demanding he pull to the curb.

Lee took his time walking up to the driver's window and was trying to contain his grin when he asked for the cameraman's license.

Diane was fuming with irritation. "You're not seriously going to give him a ticket? You guys have had your fun. You accomplished your task, she's gone now."

Lee lost his sense of humor. "What makes you think you two are exempt from the laws of the road? That was a blatant violation, and you can be sure I'm going to issue a citation." Lee walked back to his car and filled out the citation slowly. In fact, he was going to make this the neatest citation he ever submitted.

23

The front door was more than a functional way of shutting out the world; it was a piece of art. Carved into the thick, rich wood was a vineyard scene with workers among the rows of grapes and mountains in the distance. The glass near the top of the door mirrored the sky with the dramatic effect of actually creating the blue open space for the scene.

Tenny reached out to touch the carving. Her hand slid across the door as if she were reading Braille. She couldn't imagine manipulating wood until it produced such life-like forms. Tenny looked back over her shoulder to the dramatic real view enjoyed by Mr. Whittington, Senior.

Thomas Whittington's father had obviously been a successful attorney. Tenny knew that he had retired to the wine country several years ago. The vineyard below was not his livelihood but an expensive hobby. Tenny had gotten some information from police files. Now she wanted more, much more.

The doorbell chimed richly throughout the house. Tenny couldn't bring herself to knock on the masterpiece. After a few moments a man answered the door.

Henry Whittington was a tall man with beautiful gray hair that looked as soft as bunny fur. Tenny had to resist the urge to touch it. He was vigorous, with the same striking features as his son. He also had that same calm demeanor which made Tenny's heart start to race. Behind that cool, easy-going appearance, Tenny could feel something. It was the same look she had confronted at the airport, and it made her skin crawl.

Tenny pulled her badge from her belt. "Mr. Whittington, I'm Detective Mendoza and I was hoping you could spare a few minutes so that we could discuss your son Thomas."

Whittington's expression did not change. "I've already spoken with another officer and given him what information I had. I have not been close to my son for many years."

"Sir, I know you have spoken with another officer, but I'm not here to try and locate him. I was one of the investigating officers for the serial rapes, and I'm trying to understand why he was doing it."

Tenny noticed the slight surprise in Whittington's eyes when she mentioned the word "rapes." It was so small, only a momentary shift, most cops would have missed it. The other officer obviously had not told him why they were looking for his son. Yet this man must watch television and read newspapers. He must have known. Maybe it wasn't surprise that Tenny had glimpsed.

Whittington did not yield from his sentry position at the door. Tenny persisted, "The papers didn't really cover the extent of his crimes and I'm sure the other officer didn't tell you much, but Thomas' attacks were vicious and motivated by hate."

Suddenly Whittington became defensive. "My son did not hate women. Women threw themselves at him all the time. Why would he have to rape anybody? For all I know, my son is innocent and you're falsely accusing him. I have no intention of speaking with you."

The huge door was closing in Tenny's face, but she decided not to block it. Instead, she went for the longshot. "He wasn't raping everyday women. He was attacking lesbians, and he was motivated by the hate he learned from you."

The door shut, cutting off the last few words of her sentence. Tenny was betting his discomfort had been with her, not the crimes of his son. She hoped that his discomfort was no longer motivated by hate, but rather by a form of guilt.

The door opened. Henry Whittington looked like a different man as he stepped back and motioned Tenny into his home. He wasn't standing quite as tall, and there was no strength in his stare.

Tenny barely allowed them to get settled in the living room. "Thomas was speaking to his victims about stealing women from men." Whittington ran his tongue along his bottom lip and looked away. "He also accused them of destroying families." Whittington began to tap his foot on the hardwood floor and looked as if he might bolt from the room any minute.

"If the women didn't give in to his words and foreplay, he would beat them until they asked him to 'make love' to them. He wanted them to ask for it, maybe even beg for it."

Whittington looked out the big picture window. His hands shook, and he slowly moved his head from side to side as if in disbelief. Finally he spoke. "His mother left me for another woman. At least, that's what I told him. He was just a boy when she moved out. He missed her so much. I couldn't tell him that it was my fault. I couldn't explain why I beat her or made her feel like property and not the beautiful woman that she was. I couldn't make her the victim. I couldn't let him continue to want to be with her. He was my son. I wanted him with me."

He stopped for a moment, torn between trying to justify what he had done or simply, finally accepting it. When he continued, the shaking in his hands had moved to his voice. "There was another woman, and she was a lesbian. He knew her, so my story made sense to him. It was believable. A perfect excuse for my own inabilities. It just wasn't true. They were only friends.

"I never thought about how it might affect him as he grew up. We didn't even talk about it that much, and I never expressed any blatant hate for anybody."

"Why didn't his mother tell him the truth?" Tenny asked.

"Detective Mendoza, I am an excellent attorney. I manipulated the system in every way possible to keep her away from him." He spoke as if in a trance. "He wouldn't have believed her, anyway. I made sure of that."

They sat in silence. Tenny had her answer and it was making her sick. So much pain to so many people, all because of one man's insecurities. He still wouldn't look at her. Tenny wanted to go over and shake him, beat him, make him pay for what he had done. Instead, she left. This man was no longer dangerous. But she knew there were many more like him. They were the real danger.

▼

Tenny drew her gun as she approached her car. From the top of Whittington's entrance stairs she had noticed the driver's door ajar. Something moved in the front seat. Who the hell was in her car? Whittington's place was out in the middle of nowhere.

Crouching low, Tenny drew close to the vehicle. She knew that whoever was inside had entered through her door, probably headfirst, and was therefore probably lying down on the seat with their head at the passenger's side. If the person was armed, it would be more awkward to shoot overhead towards the passenger side. Tenny moved to that side and positioned herself next to the back door. She counted silently to three and sprang up, pointing her gun into the vehicle.

"Police! Don't move or I'll blow your fucking head off."

Diane Barker sat up, unaware of how close she had come to losing her life.

Tenny's anger rushed to the surface. "What the fuck are you doing in my car? Get out! Get out, damn it! Right now!"

Tenny holstered her weapon and ran around to the driver's side to grab Barker. Before the reporter could protest, Tenny threw her up against the car and handcuffed her.

"You're fucking under arrest. What the hell do you think you're doing? Who the fuck do you think you are?" Tenny wouldn't allow Barker to turn to face her.

"I'm trying to do my job. If you would cooperate with me I wouldn't have to do this. What am I under arrest for, Detective?" Barker was extremely calm.

Tenny hesitated. "You're under arrest for burglary."

Barker had been following cops around for years and knew the elements of crimes as well as they did. "It was unlocked, and I didn't take anything."

"OK, then I'll charge you with trespassing."

"Are you going to get Whittington to press charges? I don't think it will fly just because I was in your car."

Tenny was getting more and more flustered. She was about to change it to interfering with a police investigation, but she knew that was weak, too.

"Look, Detective, if you take the cuffs off me now, I won't sue you for false arrest."

That was it. Tenny either had to get away from her quickly, or lose her job for committing a justified homicide. Tenny removed the cuffs and pushed Barker away from the door.

Barker assumed her role as reporter. "What did Whittington tell you? Did you find out why?"

Tenny started the car, but as she was about to put it in reverse, Barker pulled out one of the flyers Tenny had made for the community meeting she and Steve had done weeks ago. "I found this while I was trying to track you down this morning. What a coincidence that you held it while I was out of town! You're good, Detective, but I'm starting to put the pieces together."

Barker rushed on. "I know that he was raping lesbians. That has to be why you and that other woman detective were assigned. I also know that finding him at the airport was an accident. You didn't know he was there, that's why there wasn't a game plan or sufficient backup. I'll figure it out, all of it. Then I'll tell it whether I've got it all correct or not. You *could* make sure it's right."

Tenny was torn. Would this woman really go on television with unconfirmed information? Would she find a way to confirm it? She threw the car into reverse and started to back down the drive.

Barker jogged along with her. "This is an important story. It needs to be told!" Tenny was picking up speed and leaving Barker behind. The reporter made one last, desperate attempt.

"I'm a lesbian, too, Mendoza. I think that it's important that the public knows the whole ugly truth about this case."

Tenny stopped the car. Barker came alongside her window, but couldn't make eye contact. Tenny guessed this was the first time she had ever said *it* out loud.

"What makes this story so important? What difference does it make if the victims were all lesbians or not? You're after a sensational story, that's all."

"People need to know how everybody's subtle, sometimes hidden, discrimination can help to validate one man's viciousness. They need to know that lesbians *aren't* different." Barker seemed serious, but Tenny didn't buy it.

"If it's so important that people know that lesbians aren't different, then why don't you start with the truth about yourself?"

Tenny took her foot off the brake and left Diane Barker standing in Whittington's drive. Maybe she had finally heard the last from this woman.

▼

"Do you two have me on that damn speaker phone?" Tenny was sitting in her kitchen with paperwork spread in front of her. Tomorrow she would start preparing for Thomas Whittington's return. But right now she needed to share what she had discovered today.

Steve's voice bellowed over the line, "Of course they do, Tenny. These two have every gadget you could imagine. I can't even get the stupid television on, there aren't any buttons on the damn thing. Everything's on stupid remotes." Tenny laughed.

"What're you doing over there? You're going to ruin your reputation."

"Margo's cooking tonight, so I figured if Steve came over for dinner I wouldn't have to eat leftovers for the rest of the week." Ashley must have been seated right next to the phone, because her voice was clearer than Steve's had been.

"Well, I'm glad everybody's there because I discovered some interesting information about Whittington today when I spoke to his father."

Steve, Margo, and Ashley were all at the phone waiting for answers. Tenny told them everything and when she was finished she could hear Ashley's quiet weeping. Knowing *why* didn't always make victims feel better. "I hope his father burns in hell," said Steve quietly.

Tenny continued, "I've also talked to most of the victims. It seems every one of them had traveled with a lover and they were all pretty open about their lifestyle. It's kind of ironic that it was their pride and strength that allowed him to identify what he thought of as weak, misguided women." She paused. "Ashley, you and Margo haven't travelled together, have you?"

"No," they answered simultaneously

"Then you don't fit the profile. How did he pick you out?"

"I don't know. Maybe he just got lucky."

Tenny's mind pictured Ashley lying in the hospital bed and she realized that something had been missing.

"Ashley, what happened to your mother's charm?"

"The bastard took it. He yanked it from my neck before he fled. It was all that I had left—" Ashley couldn't finish her sentence.

Steve was curious. "Why would he stop to take that, unless he had noticed it before? You don't think that he would use something as simple as a charm to judge somebody, do you?"

"It's not like we were dealing with a rational person," Margo contributed.

"There's more interesting news from my travels today. Barker is starting to put the pieces together. She's really pushing for the story, to the point of tracking me down today and going through my papers while I was talking to Mr. Whittington."

"How the hell did she manage that?" Steve inquired.

"Somehow she found me out in the middle of the wine country and she went into my unmarked."

"I hope you hooked her ass."

Tenny smiled as she thought about what would have happened to Ms. Barker if Steve had caught her.

"I did, but I had to cut her loose. I really didn't have any good charge. But as I was leaving she was telling me everything she had figured out already and trying to convince me how important the story is and how people need to know. That approach wasn't working, so then she threw out the stopper—she's a lesbian."

Margo snapped, "Bullshit! She'll say anything to get the story, Tenny."

Tenny hadn't thought of that. Would somebody be that manipulative? "I don't think so, Margo. I think she was telling me the truth. For some reason I believe her, and I also think she's being honest about feeling that the story is important. I just don't know if I agree. What do you guys think?"

"Don't give her anything, Tenny. She's too credible to go ahead with a story without confirmation from somebody." Margo was protecting Ashley and wasn't about to consider any other action.

"Steve?"

"Tenny, I don't know." He sounded confused. He knew how much he had learned from his experiences during the investigation. Maybe others could learn. Yet he didn't want to jeopardize Ashley or the other victims.

"Ashley?" Her opinion was the one that really mattered to Tenny.

"Tenny, I want it all to go away. It's over now and I just want to try to forget all the pain and hate."

Tenny made her decision. "You're right. Actually, I don't think it will be a problem. I kind of gave her a tough issue to think about. I told her—"

Tenny's call-waiting was beeping in. "Hold on a second." Tenny clicked over to take her other call.

"Tenny, turn on your TV to Channel Seven."

"Hello, Mom. What's so important on Channel Seven?"

"Just do it." Tenny's mother hung up. Whatever was on the news tonight must be good, thought Tenny. She clicked back to the group and walked out to her television.

"Hey, my mom called to tell me about something on TV right now." Tenny turned on the television and switched it to Channel Seven.

"Oh, great, it's this Barker woman." Tenny was about to shut her off when she heard what was being said.

"My professional ethic is based on the basic value of knowledge. I work hard to bring the facts to our audience because I believe that people need to know what's happening. Only with knowledge can people best react and act."

Barker looked nervous and apprehensive. Pacing from side to side, she was violating a TV reporter's primary rule. "Today, it was pointed out to me that in my search to educate and provide knowledge I have been acting as a hypocrite. I have been hiding some important information about myself."

"Shit." Tenny knew what was coming. She couldn't believe this woman's courage.

"Tenny, what is it?" Margo was sure that Barker was divulging information about the case, but she got no response from Tenny, who was hypnotized by the scene on the television.

"I am a gay woman: a lesbian." Barker stopped pacing. The words were out, and with their release went her tension. The question now was how long would the producer let her continue. Diane went on.

"Why am I telling this to anyone and everyone that happens to have this news program on? Because it's time that the minority I belong to starts being recognized as real people and not as dysfunctional queers that have no faces or personalities. It's time that the prejudice that is directed towards us is recognized as being against *people*. People of all colors, religions, professions, and economic classes. People just like everybody else." Diane couldn't believe that the red light was still on, but she had more to say.

"There's a story of prejudice and hate that I would like to share with all of you. But in order to do it correctly I needed to put a face to all the victims that happen to be lesbians. I chose to use my own, because I may be the next victim of discrimination after revealing my own homosexuality. But I'm still the same person. I'm still Diane Barker."

Tenny sat down on the couch, trying to recover from the shock. She had forgotten about the phone in her hand.

"Tenny, what's going on? We couldn't hear it all. It sounded as if she was talking about lesbians."

"I don't think she'll have time for our story anymore. She just came out on the ten o'clock news. By tomorrow morning, *she'll* be the story." Tenny was sure that phones were ringing all over the Bay Area.

"No way! You're joking, right?" All three of them were saying the same thing.

"I'm not joking with you guys. She just said it, something about how it was time to share the truth so that she could put a face to everybody's perceptions."

Steve said what was on all their minds. "That's quite a face to provide. People are going to be blown away."

"Good." Tenny couldn't help feeling proud.

There she was again, standing in the parking lot waiting for Tenny to arrive. Today was vastly different. Diane Barker had changed her own world overnight. The last night had been a long one.

She was dressed in jeans and a baggy sweatshirt. Her hair wasn't perfect and the makeup was gone. Her lean against a marked police car was not casual but tired. Watching Tenny's car pull in, Barker looked relieved. Tenny caught herself thinking how attractive Diane was, even this morning.

Tenny rolled down her window. Diane leaned down, placing both elbows on the sill.

"Well, do I get that story now?" Her voice cracked with fatigue and emotion.

"Get in, and we'll start with a cup of coffee."

▼

They sat down at a small table in the rear of the café, trying to avoid the looks that Diane imagined she was getting from everybody. A woman followed them to their table.

"Ms. Barker, I'm sorry to interrupt, but I had to tell you how proud I am of you. What you did last night set many people free in a small way. Everybody is talking about it and about homosexuality in general, and discussion is a good thing. I wanted to thank you for stepping forward and putting a face to the term *lesbian.*"

Tears came to Diane's eyes. This was the first direct public reaction to what she had done the night before. At least it was positive. "Thank you for your support."

After the woman walked away Tenny smiled at Diane, "Looks like you had a long night."

"Yeah. I guess I really didn't think things out too well before I acted. But your comment yesterday had been repeating itself in my head all evening as I prepared another story. I felt so guilty for my own attitudes and my own prejudices. I mean, I've never considered coming out before, because I didn't think my career would go anywhere if I did. I thought that the only way I could 'make it' would be to live up to the expectations of the heterosexual world."

Diane leaned forward. "But, then, yesterday, when you told me that I should start with myself, it was like somebody ripped the blindfold from my eyes. After that, what I saw was that my whole career meant nothing if *I* didn't succeed and *I* am a lesbian."

Tenny could feel herself starting to blush as Diane discussed her feelings with such passion. This woman could really express herself. Tenny laughed self-consciously. "I didn't mean to be so philosophical yesterday."

Diane smiled and slumped back in her chair, realizing that her intensity was making Tenny uncomfortable. "Well, I'm glad you were. I hope that maybe you understand me a little better now."

"I think I'm starting to. Maybe we're not as different as I assumed." Tenny shook her head in disbelief. "I can't believe I just said that about a reporter."

"Why do you dislike reporters so much?" Diane was curious.

"I guess I've never really understood what it is that you all are after. It seems that everything I read and see is so negative, depressing, and unmotivating. I always wanted the news to be something that I could look forward to, so that I could learn, and to increase our communication. Like you said last night, I wanted it to be about the knowledge and not to compete with the late night movie for action and shock value."

"Sometimes," Diane responded, "you have to shock people to get them to see or hear or listen. We put all the negative shit on the television, that's true, and every day I wait for people to say enough is enough. I wait for people to get tired of all the violence, drugs, crime, and the decay of our society. I wait for them to turn off their televisions and to go out there and put a stop to it. But in all sincerity, I don't truly know whether I'm building their tolerance up or ripping it down."

Tenny was impressed. "Maybe I've misjudged the press."

"Probably not all of its members, but you've misjudged me." Diane smiled. "Anyway, don't feel bad, because I still think most cops are assholes. But I don't include you in that group."

Tenny figured that most people didn't like cops these days, so why should Diane be any different? She couldn't resist the opportunity to mess with this woman just a little.

"Does that mean I'm not a cop or that I'm not an asshole?"

"Well, actually, you're a reformed asshole cop. But I'm sure you still need more work." Diane licked a finger and slashed her point onto the imaginary scoreboard in the air. Tenny was really starting to worry. She liked this woman.

"Oh, really, and who is going to be working on this?"

"Well, if you give me that story, then I might find some free time to work with you."

Tenny finished her coffee. "Let me give you a ride home so one of my buddies doesn't have to take your accident report."

Diane grabbed her arm. "Not so fast, Ms. Tenacity. What about my story?"

Tenny sat back down, propped her elbows up on the table, and leaned towards Diane. "I don't know, Ms. Barker. Are you still in a position to tell it?"

"Well, it was a long night," Diane sighed. "As soon as I came off the air, my pager went nuts. They pulled me right into the producer's office and started arguing about whether they should fire me or not. Shit, they dug up station policies to make sure they had the legal right to terminate me, and when they found something good, they wrote it down on the board. They did all this right in front of me." Diane's amazement was still evident.

"Finally, one of the executive producers walks in and reports that the phones had been ringing off the hook since I finished, and that most of the calls were positive. Plus, many people were calling in to say they would stop watching our news if I got yanked. Thus, here I am."

Diane smiled. "And the station wants me to go ahead with my story. I told what I had. What I thought I could get. And what I thought the story would do."

Tenny looked doubtful. "And what is that?"

Diane grew intense again. "Tenny, it can educate people. Make them feel and think. Isn't that what you told me you wanted from the news?"

Tenny finally gave in. Diane Barker had put her career on the line for something she believed in, and Tenny wasn't about to let such an unusual action go unrewarded.

▼

Tenny pulled into Diane's driveway. It hadn't been difficult to talk her into a ride home. Tenny put the car in park, but made sure to leave the engine running. She didn't want to give Diane the wrong idea.

"Here's my card. Let me put my home phone number on the back." Tenny wrote the number on the back of her card and handed it to Diane. "Give me a call when you regain consciousness."

Diane wasn't about to let this woman get away so easily.

"Actually, I'm starting to get my second wind. Why don't you come in, Detective?"

"I should get to work, you know. I still have plenty to do on this case."

"Really? What type of work? You already know why he was doing what he did. You must have gotten that yesterday from his father. Your administrators told us that he had fled the country and your partners seem to think he's probably dead. What's left?"

Tenny looked away. "All I have to do is gather the paperwork, put it in order, and finish my last supplement."

Diane looked triumphant. "Good, then you have time to come in for a moment."

Tenny gave in and followed her up the stairs to the front door. She once again found herself admiring Diane. Tenny let her mind drift back to the day before, remembered feeling Diane's body against hers as she pinned the noisy reporter to her car. She realized she wanted to feel Diane against her again.

As Diane opened the door, Tenny drew back, suddenly nervous. But Diane gently took her hand and led her into the house. Then she turned and reached behind Tenny to close the door, pushing Tenny against it. "You pushed me around yesterday," she said. "I think it's my turn." Tenny was about to object, but Diane stole the protest from her lips with a kiss.

Tenny wasn't so much surprised as overwhelmed. She wanted Diane with an intensity that terrified her.

Diane kissed Tenny again and tightened her grasp around Tenny's waist. Her mouth was warm and soft, and her tongue ran along Tenny's lips. "God, if your lips taste this good, I can hardly wait to try the rest of you." Diane hooked her hands into the front of Tenny's pants and pulled her into the house. Then, sensing the other woman's hesitancy, she turned back, slid her hands deeper into Tenny's pants, their hips together, and kissed Tenny's neck tenderly. Tenny lifted Diane's head and they kissed as Tenny gently tugged Diane's hands from her jeans.

Diane took another step into the house and Tenny followed. She was rewarded with another kiss and Diane's body pushing against her own. Then Diane moved away to the bedroom doorway. As Tenny followed, Diane lifted off her sweatshirt. Diane's breasts were a softness that Tenny had almost forgotten. She backed away. "I'm sorry. I hope someday I can understand myself enough to explain it to you, but I can't do this. Please just let me be your friend."

Surprised by Tenny's fear, Diane recovered quickly. "It's all right," she said in a soft voice. "Maybe we'll figure it out together while we get to know each other." She gave Tenny another small kiss. "I do plan to get to know you, Elizabeth."

▼

Tenny sat dazed at her desk, staring down at her hands. The band of light skin had finally disappeared from her ring finger. There was nothing left of her lost love. Nothing to remind her of the pain. Why couldn't she forget and try to trust another woman? "Shit, stupid, Diane wasn't asking you to marry her." Tenny laughed and scolded herself, but she remained on the edge of tears.

Tenny didn't have time to worry about her personal life or lack of it. There was a bigger, more important problem out there. He didn't care about anything except his lessons, and he would be back to teach her. Tenny dialed the Fraud Unit. "Frederick, have you had any luck?"

"Sure, I got the bastard! I walked over to your office a minute ago, but you didn't look like you were in a talkative mood."

"Well, I am now, so get over here."

"I got somebody on the other line. Let me get rid of them, and I'll be right over."

Frederick was in Tenny's door ten minutes later. She looked up, took a deep breath, and started to relax. "Come in, guy. It's good to actually see you. It feels like it's been forever."

"Well, girl, you know that you could walk down the hall to Fraud every once in a great while and say hello to an old friend instead of picking up the phone." Frederick came in and closed the door behind him. "First, you owe me big-time for this one. There are more hospitals and little clinics than you might think in Mexico, but there are far fewer phones."

Tenny figured that he had spent hours tracking down Whittington. "You know I would have done it myself, but you have a special skill which I don't possess."

Frederick gave her a skeptical look. "Yes, but Ms. Mendoza, why is it that you don't know the Spanish language?"

Tenny didn't make eye contact with him. It was a fact that embarrassed her as an adult. "When I was growing up, I was already different enough from all the other kids. I didn't want to be even more different. I wouldn't even let my dad speak it when I brought friends over."

"Why don't you learn it now?" Frederick wasn't going to let this drop so easily.

"Sure, I'll do that in all my free time. Just tell me what you found out. I'll grovel appropriately at your unmatchable skills some other time."

"I doubt that. Anyway, you were right as usual. He managed to get medical attention at a small free clinic not too far from the border. He didn't stay long, though, because the doctor was an American and was asking too many questions. I spoke to the doc and he thinks that Whittington probably made it." Frederick's tone grew concerned. "Tenny, the doc was really shook by this guy. He said that Whittington shouldn't have made it, but that the man had some sort of demonic drive in him. Like he wasn't about to die until he had finished something." He leaned forward and pointed his finger at Tenny.

"I want to know everything you know. I want to know how you knew he was alive. I want to know why you needed me to make all those damn calls. What's going on?"

It was time for one of Tenny's well-known exits. "I'm just doing my job, Frederick. Don't worry, I'll fill you in. Thanks for the help." Before he could respond she was out the door.

"Hey, Mom, can I give you any help out here?" Steve stuck his head into the kitchen.

"Boy, I'm not big enough to be your mother, and what is this pot full of anyway?" Tenny's mother was giggling as she peeked under the foil.

"Tenny said we were going to have a barbecue after the show, so I brought my family's famous baked beans." Steve walked into the kitchen and lifted the foil from the pot. "Another perfect batch," he announced proudly.

Tenny's mother dipped her finger in and took a taste. "Oh my goodness, these are good. Where did you learn to cook?"

Steve leaned against the counter. "I've been single for quite some time. I guess it was survival."

"My Tenny's been single and she couldn't cook to save her life." They laughed together and the sound drew the rest in from outside.

"What's so funny in here?" Tenny asked.

"We were discussing your culinary skills, honey."

"Hey, I'm going to cook today. I brought the corn. I'm going to make it myself."

Ashley had gone shopping with Tenny. "It's on the cob." She grinned. "All you have to do is boil water."

"Hey, now, be nice to my baby, that's a challenge for her."

They were all gathered at the Mendozas' house to watch Diane's show. The investigators had wanted to be together, and Tenny, especially, had wanted to be somewhere comfortable. She had invited Diane to join the gathering.

"Where's your father?" Mrs. Mendoza asked Tenny.

"He's still outside. He insisted on starting the coals now. You know how he claims that everything cooks better when there's just the right mix of hot and warm coals."

Tenny's mother herded the women out of the kitchen. "You girls go bother him then. Steve and I have talking to do." Tenny knew that meant she was going to drill him on why he was still single. She thought to herself, *Better him than me.*

They walked over to the little wall around the fish pond and sat down. "So, Ashley," Diane began, "when I was down for your interview, you were being considered for Steve's old position. What happened? Did you get it?"

"No, they decided I needed some more time in patrol. But I think they're right. I learned so much during our investigation, but mostly I learned how much I don't know." Ashley looked directly at Tenny. "Plus, I need to do the patrol doggie work for a while with the proper attitude. I expect I'll see many things that I missed in the past." Tenny smiled at her. Ashley was going to be a great cop.

"What I want to know from you, Diane," said Margo, "is if this story turned out to be all that you expected."

Diane took a deep breath. "Oh, my God, this story was so much more than even *I* suspected. I mean, I didn't have a clue of what the victims had been through. I couldn't believe how willing they were to talk about what had happened. I guess I have Tenny and Ashley to thank for that. They were the ones that organized the group interviews with the victims at both ends of the state."

Tenny interrupted. "The victims were the ones who agreed to do it, so thank them."

"They were great. When they all talked about what he had said to them and how that made them feel, for a moment I thought we should turn off the camera, but then I realized that this *was* the story." Diane shook her head in amazement. "Then they talked about how he had almost succeeded in destroying their lives. Each one of them decided for themselves that they wouldn't allow his hate to triumph. Their strength was overwhelming. They're such great women."

There was silence for a moment while they all thought about the women who had survived. Diane's voice was still filled with surprise. "But when I started the section on the investigators and the investigation, I knew that I had really uncovered a rare story. Sorry, Tenny, but Ashley and Steve stole the show. I don't think people will look at police quite the same after hearing Ashley describe her personal struggle while trying to remember. Then there was Steve; he was so honest about his prejudice and so open about how he felt while he searched for a killer who shared some of his own opinions. I think that Steve communicates the most important lesson of all."

Tenny nodded in agreement. "I tried to tell you from the beginning that I wasn't the story."

Diane winked. "Sorry, Ms. Tenacity. I know there's a story where you're concerned. One of these days I'll discover it."

Tenny threw up her arms in mock exasperation. "Is there no privacy left in this world?" Her friends joined her in laughter. Tenny thought to herself that her investigation had led her to discover something she never thought she'd find again—trust.

Steve stood at the kitchen door. "Hey, everybody, five minutes to showtime. Last one in gets the floor."

▼

The producers had thought the story was worthy of a full half-hour special and had managed to get their network to pick it up for their nightly "Newsline" program. After the program ended, they all found themselves so deeply touched that the silence in the room seemed sacred. Each of them was considering how this investigation had taught so many lessons, all of them positive. None of them the one filled with hate that Whittington had intended.

Finally Tenny's father spoke. "Diane, your story touched me as all the other stories told over the years have done, and it gives me hope. But I'm not the one that needs to be touched, and those who do probably were watching 'Wheel of Fortune'. I don't know what will make it different this time."

Steve spoke quietly. "We'll make it different."

Ashley grabbed Steve's damaged right hand. "That's right. No more great leaders, just people like us doing what we have to do to help turn around all the hate."

Tenny's father looked at her mother. "Our children here remind me of somebody from the past. They will learn how long and hard the march is towards change."

Tenny's mother had had enough intensity. "The only thing I think we should turn around right now is ourselves and head into the kitchen. We've got a meal to make." She walked over to Diane.

"Thanks for telling such a moving story about the police that people take for granted, and the strength that can be created by threat. You did a wonderful job, and you deserve every award which your industry has to offer. Now come on and help me put all this food together."

Diane followed her into the kitchen while the rest went back outside to check on the coals. Tenny's father held Tenny back momentarily. After the others had left he spoke.

"I didn't mean to sound so pessimistic. Your mother is going to kill me later. It's just that everybody shouldn't get their hopes up."

Tenny grabbed his arm and moved him towards the patio. "Sure they should, Dad. That's what it's all about—hope."

"Now that I finally have you alone, tell me why you and my daughter aren't dating and totally in love with each other?"

Diane was momentarily shocked by her frankness, but then she *was* Tenny's mother. And she had just provided Diane with an opportunity to learn more about Ms. Tenacity.

"That's a good question. I think she cares about me, and I know I'm already in love with her, but something holds us apart."

Tenny's mother frowned. "It's not something. It's somebody."

Ashley and Margo walked in to conduct their own investigation. "So Diane," said Ashley, "it's pretty obvious how you feel about Tenny. Why don't you sweep her off her feet?"

Diane looked at Mrs. Mendoza and they burst into laughter.

"What's so funny?"

"We were just discussing this. I'm willing to take suggestions from the crowd."

"Oh, girl, I don't know what to tell you," said Mrs. Mendoza. "Ever since Carter she hasn't trusted love."

Ashley was perplexed. "What does an ex-president have to do with Tenny and love?" Then she remembered the photograph which she had seen in Tenny's room.

"No, silly, Carter was her nickname," Mrs. Mendoza explained. "I don't know where she got it. Anyway, when they came apart Elizabeth let go of all the love and trust she had in her heart. I don't know if she still cares for Carter so deeply that she can't love again, or if she's just too scared to try. But the whole incident with Pearl and then Carter leaving provided Elizabeth with the excuse to hide in her work."

Diane was shaking her head. "She sure does *that* well. I don't think Tenacity is a strong enough word to describe how she approaches her job."

Mrs. Mendoza nodded in agreement. "Yes, I'll be glad when you all finally catch this Whittington creep. I don't like the idea of my baby being the bait. I hope you all are ready for him."

Ashley was shocked, but Margo found her voice first. "What are you talking about? The case is inactive. Nobody's working on it." Before Tenny's mother could respond, the four of them were out the kitchen door, Ashley in the lead.

"Tenny, what the fuck do you think you're doing? You've fucking known all this time, haven't you, and you didn't tell Steve and I that he was coming back! Who the fuck do you think you are? You're not Tenacity the Great and you can't take him by yourself!"

Tenny and Steve were seated at the picnic table and both rose as Ashley hurled across the yard, stopping inches from Tenny's face.

Tenny knew her mom had slipped, but she held her ground. Steve watched as Tenny became the ice-woman, draining all feeling from her voice. "This is no longer a police investigation, and therefore you have no reason to be involved. This is between me and him, period."

Ashley wasn't about to let Tenny end it. "That's bullshit, and you know it! If anybody owes this son-of-a-bitch anything, it's me! I want to know what's going on!"

Tenny stared straight ahead. Finally she said, "You can't be involved. I can't risk it."

Margo's anger got the better of her. "*You* can't risk it? What are you risking? What makes you so sure he'll come after you and not after Ashley again to finish what he started?"

"Look, everybody, I've got everything under control. If you try and interfere, it could be a disaster. I'm not sure where he is, or if he's even found me yet. But I am sure that if he's close, that story of Diane's will lead him right to me. Nothing can be out of the ordinary, or he'll figure out that it's a trap and disappear. He's coming after me, I'm sure of it. Let me finish this by myself. I'm the only one that can."

Ashley looked ready to attack and neither was about to back down. Steve calmly interjected, "Tenny, at least tell us what you know and what your plan is."

"All right, I'll tell you everything, but then you all have to let me do this by myself."

26

Whittington paced in the few feet of open space in the room of this so-called hotel. It felt like a penitentiary. He had easily passed back into the United States with a false ID. His strength was good and his head was clear. Most importantly, his luck was still excellent.

The only problem which he had faced was locating the woman who had challenged him, the one with the nerve to stare him down and insult his masculinity. Whittington knew she was a cop, but he no longer had access to the airline computer system. Now some stupid reporter bitch had solved his problem.

▼

Two nights ago Whittington had been sitting on his bed in the same type of hotel at the other end of the state with the television providing a static diversion in the background. He was going over how he would find that bitch cop when he had glanced up. Through the static picture of the black-and-white television, he had seen her.

Whittington jumped up off the bed and went next door. His neighbor had just stolen a new color television. When he got no response to his knock, he kicked the door in and turned on the set. There in front of his eyes was a television program about what he had done. And *her*—Detective Mendoza. As he watched and listened, he realized that they had destroyed everything he had accomplished. They were turning it all around and building strength from his lessons.

Whittington began to grow angry. This time, he intended to teach his most important lesson of all—Detective Tenacity Mendoza was going to fall, and with her all this fucked strength that these queers thought they had.

He picked up the charm he had ripped from that other dyke cop's neck. He was going to show these women that they couldn't steal power or women from men. He thought they would all get the message when he left this symbol on the raped and dead body of Elizabeth "Tenacity" Mendoza.

He began to get dressed in his black wool ninja outfit. His rental car was waiting for him, and Mendoza's house wasn't far.

▼

The tall hedge in the yard across the street threw midnight shadows from which Whittington surveyed Mendoza's two-story house. It was a nouveau-Spanish design on a corner lot halfway up a steep incline. All along the border of the yard was a low white stucco wall with a single gate leading to the front door.

Whittington slipped across the street and entered the yard. He started checking the lower windows, which were all locked, the blinds closed. There were no lights on inside and no indication that anybody was home. Whittington walked around the house to the garage and looked through the window. It was empty. Next he went to the mailbox. It was full of mail which had been postmarked at the beginning of the week. Finally, he noticed the newspapers, which some neighbor had neatly stacked near the side door to the residence.

So Mendoza wasn't home. He didn't mind. In fact he liked

the anticipation that preceded making love. Waiting for her to return was not a problem. He would be back each night until she was there. Then he would have the final word.

▼

Tenny was starting to think she was going through this whole deception for nothing. Maybe she was wrong. Maybe he wasn't coming back. The daily routine was becoming tiresome. Each evening when she came home, she parked her car blocks away. Then she went through her mail, removing only the bills which absolutely had to be attended to. She picked up her evening paper, read it quickly, then re-rolled it and put it back outside. When the sun disappeared for the day she retreated to her bedroom and finished her waking hours in complete darkness. Often this meant taking a good book into the closet and reading by flashlight for a few hours.

Although Tenny was weary of the entire routine, she knew it was the only way she could gain the advantage. Yet what if she had been doing all this for nothing? What if he wasn't coming back? What if he had already started his lessons of hate somewhere else?

These thoughts distracted Tenny as she walked around the yard, checking the soft dirt under her windows. She had re-landscaped with the express purpose of assuring that nice soft sod would be the host of beautiful flowers under each downstairs window. The sod would hold near-perfect footprints of any intruder.

As she walked past the first window and glanced at the sod, Tenny's mind was elsewhere. She was almost to the next window before she registered what she had seen.

She turned back. The sight of several footprints made Tenny's heart pound.

Tenny rushed around the rest of the house. Under each window lay the same prints. Next she sprinted to the gate, where the last clue was in place. The small black paper lay discreetly on the ground where it had fallen when he had been foolish enough to open the latch.

Tenny picked up the paper and crushed it in her hand. "Yes! I've got you, bastard." She felt only excitement. He had returned to meet her unspoken challenge. It was time for her to teach him a lesson.

Tenny dialed the dispatch center. "Hi, this is Officer Mendoza. I won't be able to make it to work today."

"Sick?"

"Yeah."

"OK, I'll notify the watch commander. Checking your messages."

Tenny waited while the communicator accessed the computerized telephone message system the department had just added.

"Nothing. I hope you feel better tomorrow."

"Can you transfer me up to Fraud?"

"No problem. Bye." Listening to the phone ring, Tenny realized it was still too early for anybody to be in the office. When the computer answered the phone, Tenny punched Frederick's extension and left a message. There was one more thing she needed him to do for her.

▼

Tenny spent the entire morning planning her trap. She acted out each possible end to her hunt. She figured out her best position within the house to be prepared for him no matter which way he chose to enter. But she knew him. She had studied him. He would enter through the side door and she would be waiting.

When she finally felt ready for him, Tenny dialed Ashley's number.

"Hi, babe." Ashley's voice was seductive.

"Ashley, what would Margo think if she knew you still had a torch burning for me?"

"Oh shit, I thought you were Margo. What's up?"

"Nothing, what are you doing?"

Ashley sounded strained. "I'm moving furniture around. I went out and bought some new stuff and now I'm trying to get everything just right."

Tenny was surprised. "You mean you're actually adding something to Margo's home?"

"Tenny, this is our home and it's time that I made it feel that way." Ashley finished shoving something heavy into place and then asked again. "So why are you calling?"

"I guess I wanted to know that you weren't mad at me anymore."

"I was never mad at you. I just don't like what you're doing. It's completely unprofessional, and that's not like you."

At last Tenny managed to explain. "Ashley, when I reacted in the airport, I didn't have time to figure out all the consequences. I was only trying not to lose him forever. Then when I realized what had happened, it got personal. I know I'm not supposed to let things become a personal battle, but that's an unrealistic expectation of cops. The pain we see, the death, the destruction, it's all personal. Sometimes when you have an opportunity to change a little piece of all that, you have to seize it."

Ashley still wasn't satisfied. "But why do you have to do this alone?"

Tenny didn't have that answer. "Don't worry, I'll be fine." She had to go. It would be dark soon.

27

Tenny's car was parked in the garage. The mailbox was empty, the newspapers had been picked up, and the outside lights were shining brightly. Whittington smiled from the shadows near her garage. He hadn't expected her back so soon, but he was ready. He hadn't slept since the night before. All he could think about was how good it was going to feel to play with this bitch until she begged him to fuck her. Then he would end it.

▼

Tenny's side door was at the end of a short hallway separating the living room and the kitchen. There was a small closet just inside the door, but Tenny had chosen not to hide there because she couldn't see his movements. Instead she stood quietly in the shadows at the far corner of the dining room. It was the darkest area of the house, and in her own black clothing she was practically invisible. She would be able to see him pass the kitchen, and then in six quick and silent steps she could reposition herself to watch him in the wall mirror she had placed in the entry area. When he started up the stairs, she would step into the entry way to confront him. He would be trapped on the staircase with nowhere to go to avoid the bullet he would get unless he did exactly what she told him.

Tenny felt the weight of the gun in her right hand—she was confident the tables of luck were about to turn.

The sound of glass breaking made Tenny jump. For a moment she nearly forgot that she had planned for this. She calmed herself quickly. Everything was going as expected.

Tenny understood how so many victims could have slept through his entrance. The small pane of glass fell almost silently to the rug below. Tenny heard the door creak open. She counted the seconds, knowing that he was inside and moving towards his lesson.

All of her concentration focused on the doorway to the kitchen. When a shadow floated by, Tenny moved effortlessly across the room to her next position. Once again, only a wall separated the hunters. Tenny had to fight her urge to just blast through the doorway and end it all right then. But this time she had a plan. She wasn't going to take any chances.

The shadow stood silently, barely casting a reflection in the mirror. Tenny stopped breathing. Why had he stopped? Did he hear her move? Could he hear her breathing? Shit, did he know that she was there? Tenny was about to lunge from her conceal-ment, convinced that he had discovered something that tipped him off to the setup. Just as her brain ordered her to lunge, he started towards the stairs. Tenny held herself in place. He started up the stairs.

▼

Ashley had been uneasy after talking to Tenny, but she couldn't figure out why. She glanced at her watch. Margo should be home soon.

"Shit, that's it. God damn her!"

Tenny was supposed to be at work today, but Ashley knew

that she had called from home. Tenny never got home that early. She was there waiting for him.

Ashley looked out into the darkness and her body started to shake. Her wrist, her ribs, and her mind ached. She could see Whittington swinging an ax through the air towards Steve. No, no! It wasn't Steve—it was Tenny. Ashley snapped her mind back and rushed to the phone. Whittington wasn't coming back to rape Tenny. This time it was death. Ashley knew he would be armed. She had to warn Tenny.

▼

Tenny slid around the wall and into the entranceway as he reached the third step. She could hear him panting. Her own breaths were deep and controlled. Her gun was leveled at his back. This was it. The end was finally here.

The sound of the phone ripped through the silence, sounding an alarm. As Whittington spun around towards the noise, he saw the dark figure standing below. The ringing echoed through Tenny's head as her eyes caught a metallic shimmer in his right hand. She flicked on the light switch, momentarily blinding them both, and dropped.

His shot flew wildly to her right as she dove left into the living room. Tenny was shocked. He had never been armed before. Her plan was useless now. Rolling to her right, she struggled to regain her balance and come out in a position to fire back.

Her own weapon was pointing in the direction she had just come from. Seconds passed and there was no confrontation. Why wasn't he attacking? Was he hiding, waiting for her to expose herself?

Then she heard him collide with the side door. He was fleeing! He wasn't supposed to run. They were here to finish it. He *couldn't* run!

Tenny sprang up and attacked the deadbolt and chain lock

on her front door. "Where the fuck do you think you live, Fort Knox?" she hissed out loud. Finally she yanked the door open.

She dove for the front steps as a bullet zipped past her. Whittington sprinted up the street.

▼

A setup! Whittington couldn't believe it. His only chance now was to escape. At the first intersection he looked over his shoulder. The detective hadn't been as smart as the television story made her out to be. Where was her backup? She had none. She had let her emotions interfere with her professional judgment, and because of that, he was going to escape. She was in pursuit, but she would never catch him. Tonight wouldn't be the final lesson for him, there would be other nights. He hadn't lost yet.

He stopped and yelled, "You stupid dyke! You'll pay for tonight!" At that moment, he heard it—an engine starting up ahead of him, then another engine off to his right and another to his left. He looked back down the hill and saw only the shadow of Tenacity standing in front of the headlights of a vehicle. Then the night exploded with the swirling of red and blue as police cars raced at him from all directions.

Whittington knew that he had been wrong about this detective. It was all about to end, but he didn't have to lose. He turned back towards Tenny and tightened his grip on his weapon. He could still kill her. He ran back towards her, bringing his weapon up.

Suddenly, a tall Black man in a police jacket burst from the shadows and tackled him before he could react.

"I'm glad you came my way, you fucker!" Frederick growled as he rolled Whittington onto his stomach. The cold steel snapped around each wrist as his arms were forced behind his back. Then several hands pulled him to his feet, and directly in front of him she stood.

There was no hate or anger as he looked into her eyes, only the strength which neither he nor others like him would ever take away. She held his gaze until he finally looked down.

"It's not over yet." Tenny dug into his pants pockets. She held up the labrys charm. "Now it is."

Photo by Devi Lynn Sanford Photography

Melanie McAllester lives and works in the San Francisco
Bay Area. She is a police officer with nine years experience,
specializing in hostage negotiations and crisis resolution
intervention. Ms. McAllester became a police officer to
discover more about people and society, and continues to
learn something new every day. She also has a Bachelor's
degree in Political Science and a Master's degree in Public
Administration. *The Lessons* is her first novel.

All The Muscle You Need, Diana McRae	$8.95
Amazon Story Bones, Ellen Frye	$10.95
As You Desire, Madeline Moore	$9.95
Being Someone, Ann MacLeod	$9.95
Cancer in Two Voices, Butler & Rosenblum	$12.95
Child of Her People, Anne Cameron	$8.95
Considering Parenthood, Cheri Pies	$12.95
Desert Years, Cynthia Rich	$7.95
Elise, Claire Kensington	$7.95
Final Rest, Mary Morell	$9.95
Final Session, Mary Morell	$9.95
Give Me Your Good Ear, 2nd Ed., Maureen Brady	$9.95
High and Outside, Linnea A. Due	$8.95
The Journey, Anne Cameron	$9.95
The Lesbian Erotic Dance, JoAnn Loulan	$12.95
Lesbian Passion, JoAnn Loulan	$12.95
Lesbian Sex, JoAnn Loulan	$12.95
Lesbians at Midlife, ed. by Sang, Warshow & Smith	$12.95
The Lessons, Melanie McAllester	$9.95
Life Savings, Linnea Due	$10.95
Look Me in the Eye, 2nd Ed., Macdonald & Rich	$8.95
Love and Memory, Amy Oleson	$9.95
Modern Daughters and the Outlaw West, Melissa Kwasny	$9.95
No Matter What, Mary Saracino	$9.95
The Other Side of Silence, Joan M. Drury	$9.95
The Solitary Twist, Elizabeth Pincus	$9.95
Thirteen Steps, Bonita L. Swan	$8.95
Trees Call for What They Need, Melissa Kwasny	$9.95
The Two-Bit Tango, Elizabeth Pincus	$9.95
Vital Ties, Karen Kringle	$10.95
Why Can't Sharon Kowalski Come Home?, Thompson & Andrzejewski	$10.95

Spinsters titles are available at your local booksellers, or by mail order through Spinsters Ink. A free catalogue is available upon request. Please include $1.50 for the first title ordered, and 50¢ for every title thereafter. Visa and Mastercard accepted.

Spinsters Ink was founded in 1978 to produce vital books for diverse women's communities. In 1986 we merged with Aunt Lute Books to become Spinsters/Aunt Lute. In 1990, the Aunt Lute Foundation became an independent non-profit publishing program. In 1992, Spinsters moved to Minneapolis.

Spinsters Ink is committed to publishing novels and non-fiction works by women that deal with significant issues from a feminist perspective: books that not only name crucial issues in women's lives, but more importantly encourage change and growth. We are committed to publishing works by women writing from the periphery: fat women, Jewish women, lesbians, old women, women examining classism, women of color, women with disabilities, women who are writing books that help make the best in our lives more possible.

spinsters ink, pob 300170, minneapolis, mn 55403-5170